Hesiod's Theogony

HESIOD'S THEOGONY

Translated,
With Introduction,
Commentary, and Interpretive Essay

by Richard S. Caldwell

Focus Classical Library
Focus Information Group, Inc.
PO Box 369
Newburyport MA 01950

CONTENTS

PREFACE

Hesiod's *Theogony* is our best and earliest evidence for what the ancient Greeks believed about the beginning of the world and its divine governance. It is a relatively short (1020 lines, in the version that we know) and straightforward account of family relationships and conflicts among the gods, culminating in the reign of Zeus and his establishment of a permanent divine order. But, underlying the genealogical lists and categorical descriptions of battles, begettings, monsters, nymphs, and remote places, the *Theogony* is also a complex and powerful statement of the connection between family status and the drive for power.

Trying to sort out the descriptive and architectural aspects of the poem from the psychological and, in a sense, philosophical is only one of several problems confronting a student of the *Theogony*. From our perspective, long after the crystallization of Greek myth into a systematic structure, the emphases in the *Theogony* seem misplaced. The major Olympian gods and goddesses, with the exception of Zeus and Aphrodite, are scarcely mentioned, while minor deities like Styx and Hekate receive lengthy portrayals and detailed attention is paid to water-nymphs, multiple-headed monsters, and the cartography of the underworld. Furthermore, the *Theogony* is perhaps the most problematic Greek text we have. We cannot say with certainty whether Hesiod wrote it, dictated it, or simply sang it, when it was composed (and when written down—the two may be separate questions), how much of it is traditional and how much original, whether Hesiod is the author of all, part, or none of it, in fact whether there ever was an actual poet named Hesiod. And these uncertainties apply not only to the poem as a whole, but even more to separate sections and even individual lines.

I have tried to help the student of the *Theogony* confront these problems by providing as much information about the poem as seemed appropriate in a book of this size. Since I presuppose from the reader knowledge neither of the Greek language nor of Greek myth, I have attempted to answer in the commentary every question which might occur to such a reader, as well as every question which, in my opinion, *should* arise. I have also made my translation as literal as possible. My motive was to avoid putting anything external between Hesiod and the reader, but I was pleasantly surprised to find that an absolutely literal translation seemed to convey the archaic, almost ritualistic, atmosphere of the original better than a less accurate rendering.

The Introduction contains a discussion of the nature and structure of the *Theogony* (including genealogical tables), a sketch of Greek prehistory, and a survey of the principal Near Eastern myths which may have influenced Greek theogonic myth. The translation and commentary are followed by an interpretive essay on the psychology of the succession myth and two Appendices: Appendix A is lines 1-201 of Hesiod's *Works and Days* (the myths of the Five Races and of Prometheus and Pandora), and Appendix B contains the theogonic sections from the Library attributed to Apollodoros.

Dante needed a relay team of guides to lead him through the cosmological adventure of the *Divine Comedy*. For the modern reader of the *Theogony*, whatever the nature of one's interest and whether one reads Greek or not, the best guide through the problems and mysteries of the text is M. L. West's definitive edition and commentary. I have used West's texts of the *Theogony* and the *Works and Days* as the basis for my translations, and my indebtedness to his commentaries will be evident from the citations in my commentary. Lines and sections of the translations which are enclosed within square brackets are those which West believes to be later interpolations in the hypothetical original texts.

I have employed the following abbreviations:

ANET   *Ancient Near Eastern Texts*,
ed. J. B. Pritchard 3rd edition with supplement (Princeton, 1969).
Ap   Apollodoros, *Library*.
Hh   *Homeric Hymns*.
Th   Hesiod, *Theogony*.
WD   Hesiod, *Works and Days*.
West, T   M. L. West, *Hesiod: Theogony* (Oxford, 1966).
West, WD   M. L. West, *Hesiod: Works and Days* (Oxford, 1978).

Internal references within this book are abbreviated as follows: *In* = Introduction; *Ps* = The Psychology of the Succession Myth; see on followed by line numbers refers to the commentary on those lines.

I have chosen to transliterate Greek names exactly, with a few exceptions: final *eta* appears sometimes as *a*, sometimes as *e*, and I have kept the traditional forms of the most familiar Greek authors (e.g., Hesiod, Homer, Aeschylus rather than Hesiodos, Homeros, Aischylos). The practice of accurate transliteration, particularly of poetry, is an increasingly frequent and commendable choice of many contemporary translations; if Zeus is not Jove or Odysseus Ulysses, then Kronos is not Saturn (or Cronus) and Ouranos is not Uranus.

All dates in this book are B.C. except where otherwise specificed.

The indices were prepared by my colleague Barry Goldfarb, and I wish to thank Professors Goldfarb, Jeffrey Henderson, and Miriam Robbins for reading the manuscript and for their helpful criticisms and suggestions.

INTRODUCTION

The *Theogony* is a mythical account of how the Greek gods came into existence, and of the relationships and conflicts between them which led finally to a permanent divine monarchy under the rule of Zeus, the supreme god and "father of gods and men." Since many of the first gods are parts of the physical universe (e.g., earth, sky, sea), the *Theogony* is also an account of how the world began. It is therefore both a "theogony" (which literally means "the origin of the gods") and a cosmogony ("the origin of the world"). But its chief purpose is clearly to trace the irresistible process which resulted in the dominance of Zeus; once the world has begun and Earth and Sky have joined together as the primal couple, a series of events is set in motion which has the reign of Zeus as its inevitable and logical conclusion.

The *Theogony* was composed toward the end of the 8th century B.C. by Hesiod, a Greek farmer-poet from the region of Boiotia. Alphabetic writing had been introduced into Greece not long before and, whether Hesiod himself put the poem in writing or dictated it to someone else, the *Theogony* is possibly the oldest surviving example of Greek written literature.

We know very little about the life of Hesiod, and nothing with certainty; although fanciful legends later arose concerning him, the only relatively reliable information we have is what Hesiod says of himself in the *Theogony* or in his other surviving work, a verse manual of ethical, mythical, and agricultural instruction called the *Works and Days*. In the latter poem Hesiod says that his father left the city of Aiolian Kyme on the eastern coast of the Aegean Sea because of economic hardship and sailed across to the Greek mainland to start a new life. He settled in the village of Askra near Mount Helicon and apparently did well enough that the inheritance he left became a matter of bitter rivalry between Hesiod and his brother Perses (*WD* 633-640). Hesiod himself became a shepherd until one day when the nine Olympian Muses, divine patronesses of the arts, appeared to him on the slopes of Helikon, gave him a laurel staff, and taught him "beautiful song" (*Th* 22-32). The song the Muses taught Hesiod is presumably the *Theogony*, and it is probably also the *Theogony* which Hesiod sang to win a prize at the funeral games of Amphidamas at Chalkis on the island of Euboia. The prize was a tripod, and Hesiod dedicated it to the Muses at the spot where they had appeared to him (*WD* 654-659).

How much of the *Theogony* is Hesiod's own invention is impossible to say, but it is virtually certain that he, like his contemporary Homer, was the heir to a long and rich oral tradition of poetry which included theogonic material. Some parts of this tradition seem to go back to the Neolithic origins of Indo-European myth, some to the Minoan-Mycenean world and its relations with eastern cultures, and some may be the result of specifically Boiotian development and more recent contacts between Boiotia and the Near East, perhaps through Euboia, which seems to have been a center of poetic activity.

Although we must suppose that theogonies existed in Greece before the time of Hesiod, these were oral literature and there is nothing we can know about them. Similarly, other theogonies may still have existed in Hesiod's own time and may even have been written, but no trace of them remains and we cannot know whether Hesiod's poem represents the usual view of how the world began, or whether it was merely one of several competing versions. The Greeks attributed theogonies to several early figures, some of them legendary, and Homer twice seems to recall a tradition in which Okeanos and Tethys, not Ouranos and Gaia as in Hesiod's version, were the primal couple, but the *Theogony* soon became the standard version and was for almost all later Greeks the true story of how the world began. As the historian Herodotos said three centuries later, it was Hesiod and Homer who taught the names and nature of the gods to Greece. We know that theogonies in both verse and prose continued to be written in Greece after Hesiod, but the fact of their almost complete disappearance indicates the superior authority which Hesiod's poem acquired. The best-known surviving alternatives to Hesiod's version are the peculiar theogony of the Orphic religion and the avian theogony of Aristophanes' comedy *Birds*, but these had ulterior purposes, religious parochialism in the case of the first and comedic parody in the case of the second. The predominance of Hesiod's account appears most clearly in the fact that the theogonic summary found at the beginning of the compilation of Greek myths called the *Library of Apollodoros* differs from Hesiod in only a few details, although it was written almost a thousand years after the *Theogony*.

It is often stated as if it were fact that Homer's *Iliad* and *Odyssey* are earlier than the *Theogony*, since the Homeric poems seem to show no knowledge of, or dependence on, the poem of Hesiod. The same argument could be used, however, to assert the priority of Hesiod, and the earliest ancient authorities seem to have believed that Hesiod was earlier than Homer. There is simply no clear evidence that either Hesiod or Homer knew the works of the other, and any resemblances between them (such as the assumption that Zeus is Kronos' son, or even shared lines and phrases) should be regarded not as borrowings or references, but as proof that both were composing within a long tradition of oral poetry which now could be preserved in writing.

The Structure of the *Theogony*

At first glance the *Theogony* seems to be a rambling and disorderly collection of myths, genealogies, and hymns of praise. Once its plan and methods are recognized, however, the structure of the whole poem is simple and apparent. The *Theogony* is a genealogical table, or family tree, in verse. It traces the lineage of two families, who happen to be comprised of gods and goddesses, over three generations, and the inherent monotony of list after list (A married B and they begot C and D; C married D and they begot E and F, and so on) is broken up by regularly inserted expansions and digressions.

The world begins with the spontaneous emergence of four divine entities (116-120). These four—Chaos, Gaia, Tartaros, and Eros—simply appear, without any source or parents, and all the other gods are ultimately descended from either Chaos or Gaia, the first two gods.

The family of Chaos is smaller in extent and importance, and is made up chiefly of the fatherless personifications born to Chaos' daughter Nyx [Night] or Nyx' daughter Eris [Strife]. Hesiod's major concern is the family of Gaia, not only because it eventually includes everyone and everything else but especially because it is her children and grandchildren whose couplings and battles will decide the question of divine rule in the universe. Ouranos, her son and husband, is the first sky-god to rule the world, his son Kronos is the second, and Kronos' son Zeus is the third, greatest, and last.

The genealogy of Gaia's descendants is understandably complicated: children are born not only parthenogenically (i.e., from a mother alone and with no father) as in the families of Nyx and Eris, but also from blood or genitals or a decapitated corpse. Also, largely because of the shortage of exogamic opportunities, there is much incest, generational lines are often crossed and confused, and some figures have multiple mates. Zeus, of course, is the best example of these characteristics; in his relentless campaign to fill the world with divine, human, and mixed offspring, he marries two of his aunts, two of his sisters, and three of his cousins (he also has illegitimate children by innumerable females, but only three, his second cousin Maia and two great-granddaughters, Alkmene and Semele, are mentioned by Hesiod).

Most of the figures who appear in the genealogies are mentioned only once and play little or no part in the generational conflict which is the main theme of the *Theogony*. The chief characters in this drama, as well as the seven wives of Zeus, are represented in the following abridged genealogy:

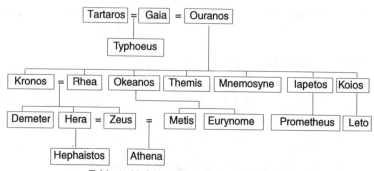

Table 1: Abridged Genealogy of the Gods

Or, if we confine ourselves to the actual succession of divine rule, the kings and queens of heaven are those of Table 2.

Table 2: Succession of Divine Rule

The genealogical patterns of the *Theogony* could be confusingly repetitive if it were not for their insertion in a narrative pattern which keeps our interest. This narrative, in turn, is embelllished with a series of digressions which clarify the structure of the whole and furthermore allow us (and presumably also the singer, in the earlier oral tradition) to catch our breath and pause before plunging once again into the complications of who begot whom and how.

The poem begins with an invocation of the Muses, the nine daughters of Zeus and Mnemosyne [Memory] who are the titular divinities of song and were regularly called upon for inspiration and guidance at the beginning of much archaic Greek poetry. There seem, in fact, to be three separate invocations (1-35, 36-103, 104-115), each of which begins with lines that sound like a poem's beginning:

> Let us begin to sing of the Muses of Helikon   1-2
> who hold the great and holy mount of Helikon
> Hesiod, let us start from the Muses, who with singing   36-37
> cheer the great mind of father Zeus in Olympos
> Greetings, children of Zeus; grant me lovely song   104-105
> and praise the holy race of immortals who always are

It is possible, but unlikely, that this tripartite division of the prologue resulted from accretion—that is, that Hesiod (or someone else) combined separate invocations from the poetic tradition and added them to the first 35 lines (which are obviously Hesiod's). A more plausible explanation of the repeated beginnings, however, would take into consideration a number of arguments in favor of the prologue's originality and integrity. First, the three sections do not duplicate one another, but treat three different subjects. The first invocation tells of the momentous vision in which the Muses granted Hesiod the gift of poetic song; the second relates the song of the Muses, their family history, names, and functions; the third is the introduction proper and summarizes the themes of Hesiod's song. Second, the length and complexity of the prologue make it an appropriate preface to a poem which may have far exceeded previous and contemporary theogonies in size and ambition. Third, the number three itself (and its multiples) has substantial significance in the *Theogony*; to cite just some instances, there are three generations of gods (twelve Titans, six Olympians, three children of Zeus and Hera), three Gorgons, three-headed Geryoneus, three-headed Chimaira, three thousand sons and three thousand daughters of Okeanos and Tethys, three Kyklopes, three Hundred-Handed, three Horai, three Moirai, three Charites, and, of course, three times three Muses.

The third invocation leads directly into the body of the poem, which begins with the spontaneous appearance of Chaos, Gaia, Tartaros, and Eros (116-122). By their emergence from nothing, without source or parents, these four are separated from everything which follows. With the appearance of Eros [Desire], however, the situation changes and all subsequent production will be reproduction; everything which comes into existence will have a parent, or parents, or some kind of source.

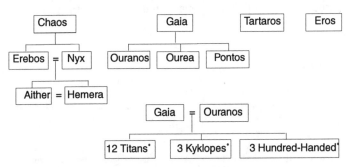

Titans: Okeanos, Koios, Kreios, Hyperion, Iapetos, Theia, Rhea, Themis, Mnemosyne, Phoibe, Tethys, Kronos.
Kyklopes: Brontes, Steropes, Arges.
Hundred-Handed: Kottos, Briareos, Gyges.
Table 3: Original Gods and Descendants of Gaia and Ouranos

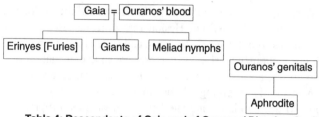

Table 4: Descendants of Gaia and of Ouranos' Blood or Genitals

At this point Chaos and Gaia begin producing offspring parthenogenically (123-132). Chaos gives birth to Erebos [Darkness] and Nyx [Night], who unite to produce their opposites, Aither [Brightness] and Hemera [Day]. Gaia [Earth] gives birth to Ouranos [Sky], the Ourea [Mountains], and Pontos [Sea], then mates with her son Ouranos to produce the twelve Titans, the three Kyklopes, and the three Hundred-Handed (133-153, see Table 3).

Hesiod here interrupts the genealogical presentation to tell the story of the family of Gaia and Ouranos (154-210). As each of their children is born, Ouranos imprisons him or her in the body of their mother Gaia. Finally Gaia is in such discomfort that she makes a great sickle of adamant and asks her sons to punish their father. All are too frightened to speak but Kronos, the youngest, who takes the sickle from his mother and castrateshis father during his parents' sexual embrace. A number of children are born from the drops of Ouranos' blood which fall on the earth, and the severed penis itself, which Kronos throws into the sea, is transformed into the goddess Aphrodite. (See Table 4)

The genealogy of the descendants of Chaos is now resumed and followed to its completion (211-232, see Table 5). Nyx, who had earlier mated with Erebos, turns to parthenogenic reproduction and bears a brood of fif-

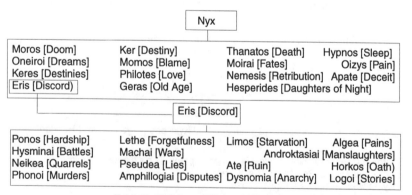

Table 5: Children of Nyx and Eris

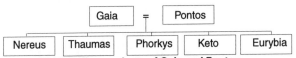

Table 6: Descendants of Gaia and Pontos

teen abstractions, most of them associated with darkness and conflict. Her youngest child Eris [Discord] follows her mother's example and by herself produces fifteen similar beings.

Having finished this line of descent, Hesiod returns to the children of Gaia, this time to the collateral line descended not from Ouranos but from another son, Pontos [Sea]. This line is also followed to its end and consists chiefly of sea deities and hybrid monsters (233-336).

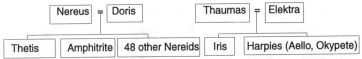

Table 7: Descendants of Nereus and Doris and of Thaumas and Elektra

Nereus, the "old Man of the Sea," marries Doris, a daughter of the Titans Okeanos and Tethys, and they are the parents of the Nereids, fifty nymphs of the sea. Thaumas marries Elektra, a sister of Doris, and they produce Iris [Rainbow] and the two bird-woman Harpies.

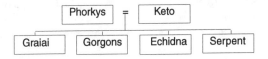

Graiai: Pemphredo, Enyo
Gorgons: Sthenno, Euryale, Medousa
Table 8: Descendants of Phorkys and Keto

Phorkys marries his sister Keto and they produce a first generation of monstrous progeny (Table 8).

The Gorgon Medousa's two children by Poseidon, born at the instant of her decapitation by the hero Perseus, are the winged horse Pegasos and the warrior Chrysaor. Chrysaor then marries Kallirhoe, another daughter of Okeanos, and their son is the three-headed Geryoneus (Table 9).

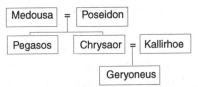

Table 9: Descendants of Medousa and Posidon

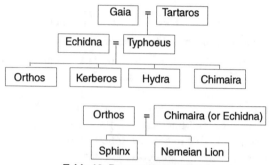

Table 10: Descendants of Echidna

Echidna, who is half-woman and half-serpent, unites with Typhoeus, son of Gaia and Tartaros and the most fearsome monster of them all, to produce four additional monsters. Her oldest child is Orthos, the dog of Geryoneus, who is the father of two more monsters by his sister Chimaira or his mother Echidna (Hesiod's reference is ambiguous, Table 10).

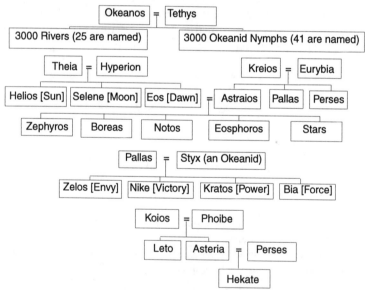

Table 11: Families of the Titans

Hesiod now returns to the families of the Titans (337-382); since Kronos is the youngest Titan, he recounts the children of Okeanos and the other older Titans before finally coming to Kronos and resuming the succession myth. The Titans Okeanos, Hyperion, and Koios marry their sisters Tethys,

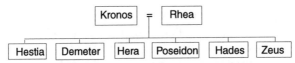

Table 12: Descendants of Kronos and Rhea

Theia, and Phoibe, while Kreios marries his half-sister Eurybia (daughter of Gaia and Pontos)(Table 11).

After a short digression on the status of the Okeanid Styx (383-403) and a hymn in praise of the goddess Hekate (411-452), Hesiod comes to Kronos, successor to Ouranos as ruler of the sky, and his wife Rhea (453-506) (Table 12).

Kronos, who knows from his own experience that he cannot prevent being overthrown by repeating the strategy of his father Ouranos and keeping his children inside their mother's body, chooses instead the other alternative. He swallows each child as it is born and thus, by keeping the children in his own body rather than in that of his wife, expects to avoid the complicity of his wife in a potential rebellion. His attempt is doomed to fail, however, as his parents have predicted. When Rhea is about to give birth to Zeus, her youngest, she asks Gaia and Ouranos for help; they send her to Crete, where Gaia arranges for the nurture of Zeus without the knowledge of Kronos, while Rhea gives to Kronos a huge stone, wrapped in baby's clothing, to swallow.

When Zeus grows up he releases his uncles, the Kyklopes and Hundred-Handed, from their prison within the earth, and joins his brothers and sisters, whom Kronos has been forced to disgorge, to begin the great war between the gods and the Titans.

The succession story is now interrupted so that Hesiod can finish the genealogy of the Titans (507-520). The three members of the first Titan generation whose stories remain to be told are Iapetos, Themis, and Mnemosyne, and the reason for their deferral is the involvement of them or their descendants with Zeus, who must therefore be brought into the scene. The sons of Iapetos (Table 13), most notably Prometheus and Atlas, will be punished for their offenses against Zeus, and Themis and Mnemosyne will become wives of Zeus.

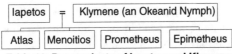

Table 13: Descendants of Iapetos and Klymene

The reasons for Zeus' punishment of Atlas and Menoitios are unclear, but the conflict between Zeus and Prometheus is described in detail (521-569). When the gods and men met at Mekone to determine the distribution of sacrifices, Prometheus had deceived Zeus into taking the inferior portion, and Zeus retaliated by withholding from men the use of fire. Prometheus then stole fire and carried it to men in a hollow reed, whereupon Zeus punished mankind by ordering the creation of Pandora, the first woman, and sending her to men as the source of great evil (570-589). Prometheus himself was bound with inescapable chains and tortured by an eagle who ate his liver daily, until eventually Zeus allowed his son Herakles to kill the eagle and release Prometheus from his suffering. The digression ends with a misogynistic tirade against women and the admonition that no one, not even Prometheus for all his cleverness, can surpass the mind of Zeus (590-616).

The conflict between the Titans and the Olympian gods is now rejoined (617-721). The war has been raging for ten years with no end in sight until Zeus, at Gaia's advice, releases the Hundred-Handed from their imprisonment. Revived by nectar and ambrosia, the food of the gods, they enter the war and the entire universe is shaken by the climactic struggle. Zeus now attacks with his lightning bolts, setting the earth and ocean on fire, and the tide of battle is turned. The Olympian gods under Zeus now rule the world, and the Titans are bound and confined in Tartaros.

In a lengthy digression (722-819), Hesiod now describes the underworld, with special emphasis on the role of the goddess/river Styx, whose primal water is the libation by which the gods swear oaths. The relevance of this long passage to the poem as a whole has often been questioned, but the logical transitions to, from, and within it are not difficult or forced. After the defeat of the Titans, the place of their punishment is appropriately described, and the portrayal of Tartaros is then expanded to include the entire underworld. The river Styx is a prominent feature of the underworld and the goddess Styx has already appeared as the oldest (777) and most eminent (361) daughter of Okeanos and as an important ally of Zeus in the war against the Titans. Furthermore, she is a powerful non-Olympian goddess whose function and privileges in the underworld parallel those of Hekate, whose influence (according to Hesiod) extends throughout the world except for the underworld. Earlier in the poem both Styx and Hekate were said to have received significant gifts from Zeus (399, 412) and to have retained their previous prerogatives when Zeus came to power; now Styx is honored in her dominion, where she is invoked by the gods, as earlier Hekate had been honored and invoked by men. It seems, therefore, that Styx is the counterpart of Hekate in the underworld in the same way that Hades is the infernal counterpart of his brother Zeus.

The next episode of the *Theogony* deals with the battle between Zeus and Typhoeus (820-885), a conflict which recalls the earlier war between Zeus and the Titans. Tartaros, whose description began the previous section, appears again in two different forms, as the father of Typhoeus and as the place where Typhoeus will be punished alongside the Titans. Again the world is shaken to its foundations and the earth is set on fire by the terrible struggle, and again Zeus is victorious. With this triumph the rule of Zeus is officially established; he determines the positions of the other gods and then turns to the business of procreation, his principal concern henceforth.

Hesiod now lists the seven goddesses who become wives of Zeus and the offspring who result from these unions (886-923). Zeus first marries the Okeanid Metis, but when she is about to give birth to Athena, Zeus learns that her second child is fated to replace him as king of gods and men. Unlike Kronos, who swallowed his children, Zeus deals with the potential threat by swallowing his wife.

The second wife of Zeus is his aunt Themis, who bears the three Horai [Seasons] and the three Moirai [Fates]. She is followed by the Okeanid Eurynome, who produces a third triad, the Charites [Graces]. The fourth wife is Zeus' sister Demeter, and their daughter Persephone will become the wife of Hades. Next is another aunt, Mnemosyne, the mother of the nine Muses. Sixth is Leto, daughter of the Titans Koios and Phoibe and mother of Apollo and Artemis.

Zeus' seventh and final wife is his sister Hera, and their children are Hebe, Ares, and Eileithyia. At this point Zeus gives birth from his head to

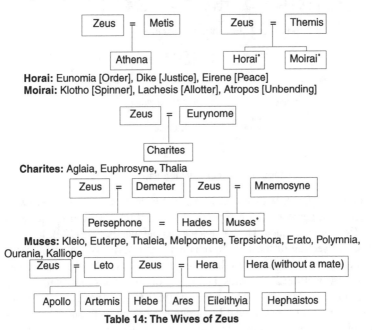

Horai: Eunomia [Order], Dike [Justice], Eirene [Peace]
Moirai: Klotho [Spinner], Lachesis [Allotter], Atropos [Unbending]

Charites: Aglaia, Euphrosyne, Thalia

Muses: Kleio, Euterpe, Thaleia, Melpomene, Terpsichora, Erato, Polymnia, Ourania, Kalliope

Table 14: The Wives of Zeus

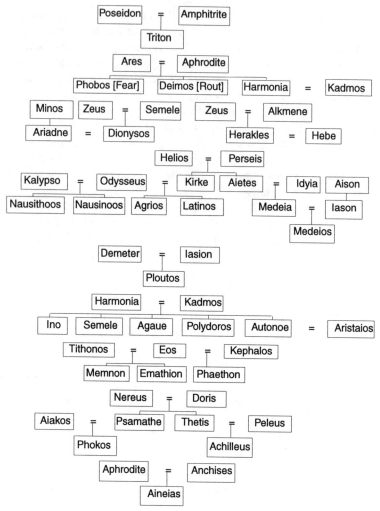

Table 15: Other Genealogies

the goddess Athena, with whom Metis had been pregnant when he swallowed her. Angered by the independent procreation practiced by her husband, Hera now produces Hephaistos parthenogenically (927-929).

The last section of the *Theogony* is a series of brief genealogical mentions beginning with Zeus' brother Poseidon (his other brother Hades has no children) and Zeus' son Ares, and going on to various unions involving gods (including Zeus) and then goddesses (930-1020). The order of presentation is based on a patriarchal hierarchy, according to the divinity of father, children, and finally mother. The entire passage forms a transition to a lost genealogical poem attributed to Hesiod, the *Catalogue of Women*, which told of families descended from the unions of mortal women with gods. The last two lines of our *Theogony* introduce the subject of the *Catalogue*; the last 100 or so lines of the *Theogony*, as well as the *Catalogue* whose fragments have survived, were written by an imitator of Hesiod, perhaps during the 6th century B.C.

After Hesiod the origin of the gods seems to have held much less interest for Greek myth than mortal heroes and the relationships of heroes with one another and with the gods. The divine world becomes a kind of background (sometimes, as in the *Iliad* and certain tragedies, a background with a mirrored surface) to the world of heroes and their adventures. This relative lack of interest in theogonic matters may help answer two questions in regard to the *Theogony*. First, the virtually unchallenged authority of Hesiod may be due not only to the date at which he wrote (that is, to his position as both the last in a long oral tradition and the first theogony-poet to commit his poem to writing), but also to the shift in attention and emphasis from divine to primarily human matters (a shift which took place long before either Hesiod or Homer). Second, the apparently excessive number of lines spent on such matters as the description of the underworld, the catalogues of nymphs and monsters, the praise of the Muses, Styx, and Hekate, and the complaint against women (which together make up half of the poem) may be due to this shift and to the simple fact that these were not the usual subjects of mythology. The *Theogony* is basically a logistical poem, and its purpose is setting the pieces of divine machinery in place and in order. The inherent tediousness of this project needs to be relieved, but the means by which this relief is accomplished is hymnic or descriptive material rather than episodes from heroic myth. The chief characteristic of all the digressions from the main business of the poem (the genealogies and the succession story) is their static nature. Catalogue, hymn, description, and diatribe are essentially motionless elements which divide into separate segments the chronological and unilinear movement of genealogy and generational conflict.

This does not mean, however, that the digressions are irrelevant to the larger purpose of the poem. Nymphs and monsters are often as necessary as the gods themselves in the setting and plots of heroic myth, and it is the *Theogony* which provides this setting. The underworld description is significant not only because the underworld is where most of the chief actors in the succession drama are lodged either temporarily or permanently, but also because it has an inevitable, if potential, importance for the lives of the poem's human audience (who may never see Olympos, but will certainly spend time in Hades). The wish to establish a human contact is understandable in a poem specifically concerned with the non-human world, and may also explain the attention given to the Muses, Styx, and Hekate; they are divinities who, in Hesiod's view, directly affect human life and death.

The same is true of the long central panel of the poem, the two-part digression on Prometheus and Pandora. Both phases of the conflict between Prometheus and Zeus, the sacrificial dispute and the theft of fire, are concerned with crucial factors in human existence, the first with mankind's role in its relationship with the gods, and the second with the institution and value of civilization itself. The final outcome of this conflict, the creation of Pandora, turns a conflict between deities into a central fact of human life, the battle of the sexes. The ambivalence of the gods themselves, their often quixotic alternation between benevolence and destructiveness, is reflected in the "lovely evil" (585) of woman.

We may note in passing that the same explicit use of mythical digressions to characterize human life is found in Hesiod's other extant poem, the Works and Days. Here there are two such digressions, related one after another at the beginning of the poem: the first tells the story of Prometheus and Pandora, a bit differently than the *Theogony* version, and the second is the myth of the Five Races through which mankind has descended. The aim of both digressions is to trace the background and causes of the present human situation, to explain the grim conditions of life (in Hesiod's pessimistic view) in terms of mythical antecedents. If life is full of troubles, evil, and disease, it is because of Pandora (and, ultimately, Prometheus and Zeus); and if mankind has never-ending labor and grief, with strife and violence as the ordinary state of human relationships, this is because the men of Hesiod's time are an "iron race," living in the last and worst of the five mythical ages.

The details of the genealogies and the psychological meaning of the succession story will be discussed in the Commentary and Interpretation, respectively. Before we leave the subject of the *Theogony*'s structure, however, there is one matter, alluded to earlier, which should now be treated in greater detail: the inevitable, logically necessary process which leads from the union of Gaia and Ouranos to the permanent sovereignty of Zeus.

It will be helpful first to summarize the succession myth. Gaia marries her son Ouranos and they have eighteen children, whom Ouranos does not allow to emerge from their mother's body. Gaia, distressed by this, somehow gives her youngest son Kronos an adamantine sickle, which he uses to castrate his father during the act of intercourse. Kronos now releases at least eleven of his brothers and sisters, the Titans, and becomes king of the gods; whether he also releases the three Kyklopes and three Hundred-Handed, and then re-confines them, is unclear in Hesiod's text. Kronos marries his sister Rhea, an earth-goddess like her mother, and they have six children, the first generation of Olympian gods. However, as each of his children is born, Kronos swallows him or her. Finally, when Rhea is about to give birth to Zeus, she gives Kronos a stone, disguised as a baby, to swallow, and Zeus is secretly born and raised in Crete. When he has grown to maturity, Zeus leads and wins a great war against his father and the other Titans, aided by the released Kyklopes and Hundred-Handed and by his fellow Olympians, whom Kronos has been forced to disgorge through a trick of Gaia. Zeus now becomes the third king of the world and marries first the Okeanid nymph Metis. While she is pregnant with Athena, Zeus learns from his grandparents that Metis' second child is fated to be a son who will rule over gods and men. Zeus prevents the birth of this child by swallowing Metis, gives birth to Athena from his own head, and secures his permanent reign.

We may begin with an obvious question: why does Ouranos confine his children in their mother's body? His son Kronos and grandson Zeus will naturally take steps to prevent being overthrown, because they know what happened to their predecessors, but what prior knowledge could Ouranos possibly have which might cause him to suspect that one of his children will try to usurp his position? Hesiod says merely that Ouranos "hated" his sons because they were "most terrible" (155), but how could he know this if the children are not even allowed to be born? Perhaps Ouranos heard the children misbehaving inside their mother—there is actually a parallel for this in a Babylonian myth, as we shall see—but a more reasonable explanation is available. Gods, like children, tend to rely on their own past experiences to determine their present behavior, and Ouranos has a good reason from his past to fear his children. This reason is the fact that he married his mother; if Ouranos did this (and, at this early point of cosmic history, he knows of no alternate behavior), his children will want to do the same, and therefore he must suppress them. Now Ouranos must make a decision. His children, being immortal, cannot be killed, but must be imprisoned, and there are only two possible locations: either in the sky (that is, in himself) or in the earth (that is, in their mother). Ouranos chooses the latter, and it is the wrong choice; his son Kronos, thanks to the intervention and complicity of Gaia, castrates and replaces his father.

Kronos now faces a similar situation. If he does not renounce sexual activity (which would be equivalent to renouncing his position as paternal sky-god), he must arrange that his sons will not do to him the same thing he did to his father. The decision he takes is clearly derived from his memory of what had happened to Ouranos and from his intention to avoid a similar fate by adopting a different strategy. In order to prevent his sons from overthrowing him, he thinks, he cannot keep them in their mother's body, but must keep mother and sons separate as well as suppressing the

sons themselves. Therefore Kronos chooses the strategy Ouranos had re-
jected, and puts his children into his own body rather than into their
mother's.

The choice of Kronos is logically quite simple. Since he cannot kill his
children and does not want to adopt the failed strategy of Ouranos, the only
option remaining—an obvious but significant emendation of Ouranos' tac-
tic—is to imprison either his children or his wife in the other parental body,
in himself rather than in Rhea. Kronos must swallow either his children or
his wife, and he chooses the former presumably because the alternative
would not only leave his children running free but also would deprive him
of his sexual partner. In fact, he would have to swallow his wife immediately upon the birth of their first child (and, I imagine, hope that this first
child is a daughter).

The oracular warning given to Kronos by his parents (463-464) is therefore superfluous. It merely reminds him of his own experience and tells
him nothing new, except that he will make the wrong choice. Zeus in turn
will be faced with the same situation and the same choices, but he will
choose correctly; that is, he will swallow his wife instead of his children.
By electing this strategy (which involves no great thought, since it is the
only remaining alternative), Zeus will establish himself as the most notable
exception to the underlying law of myth, as well as of life, that fathers are
destined to be replaced by their sons, and he will exemplify the male wish
that what he wanted to do to his father will not be done to him in turn.

Therefore we know, even before we are told, that Zeus will have to
swallow a wife. He has learned from the fates of Ouranos and Kronos that
to put his children in either his wife's body or his own is not a satisfactory
solution, and he also realizes that the real enemy is not so much the children as the wife. Zeus must either repeat the mistake of his ancestors
(which he cannot do, or someone else would now be ruling the sky), or he
must put his wife, not his children, inside himself. There is no other alternative.

Thus the Hesiodic tradition created a succession myth of striking psychological logic. This primal story of generational rivalry, marital conflict,
and maternal preference is reduced to a series of clear-cut either/or choices
which lead inevitably to the accession of Zeus as the greatest and permanent sky-god. The strict logic of the process and the certainty of its conclusion are embellished by several imaginative hints of Zeus' final victory. For
example, even while the war between Zeus and the Titans is in progress,
Hesiod pauses to tell the story of Zeus' triumph over Prometheus. And in
this story Hesiod almost certainly alters the tradition he had received,
which probably told of Zeus really being deceived by Prometheus and
choosing the wrong portion. In the *Theogony*, however, Hesiod substitutes

a version in which Zeus—who will later, on a more important occasion, make the correct and only decision—now merely pretends to choose wrongly.

Greece Before Hesiod

Hesiod and Homer did not invent writing, nor did they invent literature, but their works are the earliest surviving examples of Greek literature written down in the alphabetic script which the Greeks borrowed from Phoenicia, probably during the 8th century or shortly before. Once before the Greeks had possessed a method of writing, the syllabic script known as Linear B which the Myceneans adopted from Minoan Crete. The use of Linear B, however, seems to have ended with the destruction of Mycenean civilization 500 years before Hesiod, and in any case the surviving Linear B material contains nothing literary or mythological except for the names of a few gods, some of them familiar.

It is not only written literature which first appeared at the time of Hesiod; Greek history itself can be said to have begun during the 8th century. Everything before this time, despite the brief presence of Mycenean writing, is prehistoric in the sense that virtually all we know about the way people lived, including their religious beliefs and myths, is based on the physical remains studied by archaeologists and not on written records. For this reason almost everything said in the following survey of Greek prehistory is probable at best; the present state of our knowledge does not allow certainty in most matters, and in some of the most important does not even guarantee probability. This is not true, at least to the same extent, of the ancient Near East, where written records and literature existed long before the arrival of the first Greek-speaking people in Greece at the end of the third millennium. Nevertheless the question of influence and exchange between Greece and the East during the prehistoric period is still largely a mystery.

The Greek language is Indo-European; that is, it belongs to the large family of languages derived from a single language spoken by a hypothetical people who lived in northeast Europe or northwest Asia during the Neolithic period. In irregular waves of migration from the beginning of the third millennium to the middle of the second, descendants of this people spread throughout Europe and into central Asia as far east as India. One branch of these Indo-European nomads, who spoke an early form of the language we now know as Greek, entered the mainland of Greece around the beginning of the second millennium. They presumably brought with them both poetry and a polytheistic religion in which the chief god was associated with fatherhood and the sky, since these are elements of the general Indo-European tradition. In Greece they met, probably conquered, and merged with a native people, the early Helladic culture of the beginning of the Greek Bronze Age; before the coming of the Greeks, metallurgy had been introduced into Helladic Greece from the east, just as agriculture, the domestication of animals, and the painting of pottery had come earlier to Greece from Mesopotamia through Asia Minor. We know hardly anything about Helladic religion, of which only a few figurines have survived; whether it may have resembled the religion of nearby Minoan Crete remains a guess.

When the first Greeks entered Greece, one of the great civilizations of the ancient world was already flourishing on the island of Crete to the south. This culture, known as Minoan after Minos, the mythical king of Crete, had been in contact with the Near East and Egypt during the 3rd millennium; thanks to these contacts (which were to increase greatly during the 2nd millennium), a favorable climate, and a protected location, the Minoans had developed a prosperous civilization with large unfortified cities, great royal palaces, and spectacular refinements in art and architecture. The Minoans also possessed writing in the form of a pictographic or hieroglyphic script which developed later into Linear A, the syllabary which the Mycenean Greeks adopted to write Greek. Since neither Minoan scripts have been deciphered, all our evidence for Minoan religion is pictorial and conjectural. A goddess (or probably goddesses, who may yet represent different aspects of one goddess), presumably associated with the earth and fertility, seems to be the dominant figure; male figures who may be gods appear, and later myths such as Hesiod's story of the infancy of Zeus on Crete (*Th* 468-484) may point to a Minoan myth of a son or consort (or both) of a goddess.

Within a few centuries of their arrival, the Greek rulers of the mainland came squarely under the influence of the Minoans. The power and cultural sophistication of the mainland increased rapidly through the Middle Helladic period and reached its height during the late Helladic period, the 16th through the 13th centuries. Meanwhile the Minoan civilization, at its greatest during the 17th and 16th centuries, went into decline after the destruction of the palaces, caused perhaps by the eruption of the volcanic island Thera around 1450.

The Late Helladic period, the final phase of the Bronze Age on the Greek mainland, is most commonly named the Mycenean period, since the city of Mycenae in the Peloponnese seems to have been the most important Mycenean center (an assumption strengthened by the pre-eminence of Mycenae and its king Agamemnon in the myths of the Trojan War). The chief Mycenean cities—Mycenae, Tiryns, and Argos in the Argolis, Pylos in Messenia, Thebes and Orchomenos in Boiotia, Iolkos (modern Volos) in Thessaly, Eleusis and Athens in Attica, as well as Knossos on Crete, which was taken over by the Myceneans during this period—all play a significant role in later myth, and it is this period which provides the setting for much of Greek myth as it was later known to Hesiod and Homer.

Minoan influence on Mycenean civilization is so extensive that the few exceptions stand out clearly. There is nothing in Crete like the battle scenes in Mycenean art, or the enormous Cyclopean fortifications which protect the Mycenean citadels (the archaeological term is derived from myths crediting the one-eyed giants called Kyklopes with building these walls; post-Mycenean Greeks did not believe that ordinary mortals could have lifted the great stone blocks). Mycenean frescoes, jewelry, pottery painting and shapes, and architecture (with such exceptions as the distinctive Helladic room-style called the *megaron*) imitated Minoan models so closely that it is often difficult to tell them apart. Whether the same assimilation applied to religion and myth is impossible to say; the iconographic evidence shows great similarity, but the absence of literary records makes these pictorial data difficult to interpret. The figure of a bull, for example, appears everywhere in the Minoan remains—on buildings, frescoes, pottery, and jewelry and in sacrificial, ritual, and athletic contexts—and the bull is very prominent in later Greek myths concerning Crete, but the exact connection between artefacts and myth is impossible to establish. In the case of Mycenean culture we have the advantage of written records in a known language, but since the Linear B tablets are almost entirely inventories and accounting records of the religious and political bureaucracy, all they can tell us are the names of some deities and the facts that sacrificial cults existed and that the religious system was highly organized.

Names on the Linear B tablets which correspond with gods and goddesses in later Greek religion include Zeus, Hera, Poseidon, Hermes, Enyalios (a double of Ares), Paiaon (an epithet of Apollo), Erinys (an epithet of Demeter, as well as the singular form of the three Erinyes or Furies), Eleuthia, and perhaps Athena, Artemis, Ares, Dione, and Dionysos. In addition, there is a goddess, or many goddesses, called Potnia ("lady" or "mistress"), a name occurring usually but not always with some qualification: Potnia of horses, Potnia of grain, Potnia of the labyrinth, etc. Finally there are several deities whose names do not appear later, such as Manasa, Drimios the son of Zeus, and Posidaija (a feminine form of Poseidon). The tablets, on a few of which these names appear, were found in great number at Knossos and Pylos and in smaller quantities at Mycenae and Thebes; they were preserved by the fires which accompanied the destruction of these sites during the 14th through 12th centuries.

The end of Mycenean civilization coincided with general disruption in the eastern Mediterranean area and may be due, at least partially, to the raids of the mysterious "Sea Peoples," who appear most prominently in Egyptian records. A major role may also have been played by the movement into central Greece and the Peloponnese of new groups of Greek-speaking peoples from the northwest, the "Dorian invasion." Only Athens and its surrounding area, and a few isolated places in the Peloponnese, escaped destruction.

Most survivors of this turbulent period probably remained in Greece under the new Dorian regime, but the level of culture changed radically; writing, building in stone, and representational art disappeared, and cultural depression and poverty were widespread, especially in the century or two immediately following the Mycenean collapse. A Mycenean group fled to the island of Cyprus soon after the Dorian invasion; they were followed, toward the end of the 2nd millennium, by large-scale migrations from the Greek mainland to the eastern Aegean islands and the coast of Asia Minor. Aiolians from Boeotia and Thessaly moved into the northern part of this area, Ionians (a mixed group chiefly from Attica and Euboia, but perhaps including temporary refugees in Athens from other parts of Greece) occupied the central section, and Dorians settled in the south, including Crete. A cultural revival began in Athens around 1050, marked by a distinctive pottery style called Proto-Geometric, and gradually spread throughout the Greek world. Other than changes in the Geometric pottery series and a great increase in the use of iron during the 11th century, however, there is little we can say about Greek higher culture during the period 1200-800, appropriately called the "Dark Age" of Greece.

Nevertheless there seems to have been an extended period of relative calm and stability during the second half of the Dark Age, which resulted in a substantial increase in both population and prosperity by the end of this period and the beginning of the Archaic period (8th-6th centuries). By the time of Hesiod, during the first century of the Archaic period, Greece had entered into a cultural and economic revival of large proportions. Over-population was an important factor not only in political and economic change but also as an impetus for a great colonizing movement which spread Greek culture throughout and beyond the central and eastern Mediterranean during the Archaic period. More significantly, colonization introduced Greece to other cultures, and this acquaintance was accelerated by the rapid expansion of Greek trading relations, particularly with the Near Eastern civilizations of Syria and Phoenicia. An increasingly powerful merchant class arose, generating further political and economic change, and a wealth of new ideas poured into Greece from overseas, including coinage, the Orientalizing pottery style, the alphabet, and knowledge of eastern customs and myths. We cannot know to what extent Hesiod participated in these Archaic developments; the legends which appeared later about his travels cannot be verified, and the only real evidence we have is what is contained in the surviving poems. The only place we know he visited is

Chalkis on Euboia, the long island which runs along the eastern borders of Attika, Boiotia, and Thessaly, scarcely ever more than a stone's throw from the mainland. Euboia was almost certainly an important center of cultural and poetic activity at Hesiod's time and before, and, because of its close contacts with the Near East, it was a place where eastern ideas could affect Aiolic and Ionic poetic traditions.

Hesiod and the Theogonic Tradition

It is possible, but quite unlikely, that Hesiod invented either all of the *Theogony* or none of it. The truth, as far as it can be known, is probably that he used the recent innovation of writing to compose a poem for the Chalkis competition which drew heavily on an old tradition of oral theogonic poetry, but also contained Hesiod's major and original contributions in both arrangement and content. The question of what is original and what is inherited from the poetic tradition is difficult and complicated, and ultimately impossible to resolve byond any doubt. The matter of the Greek theogonic tradition must be left at that, even though the tradition probably extends for over a thousand years before Hesiod, for the simple reason that not a word of earlier theogonies remains.

The question of the influence of Near Eastern theogonies on Hesiod is quite different, since several of these theogonies have been preserved. Here again, however, we must distinguish between the *Theogony* of Hesiod and the Greek theogonic tradition. We can compare Near Eastern theogonies to Hesiod and note differences and similarities, but we cannot know whether Near Eastern influence affected Hesiod directly or whether it affected the Greek tradition, perhaps centuries earlier, which Hesiod inherited.

There is no doubt that there are connections between the theogonic traditions of Greece and those of the Near East. The similarities are too obvious and complex to have originated independently. Furthermore, it is generally agreed that the direction of influence went from east to west, although even this assumption cannot be stated with absolute certainty; despite the fact that the earliest Near Eastern theogonies antedate the presence itself of Greeks in Greece, it is possible that both traditions developed independently from a common pre-Bronze Age source.

The most likely conjecture is that there was a native Greek theogonic tradition as early as the first Indo-European invasion of Greece at the beginning of the 2nd millennium, and that this tradition was subject to the possibility of Near Eastern influence at virtually any time throughout (or even before) the Bronze Age, Dark Age, and early Archaic period. The two most likely occasions on which this influence might have been felt are the Minoan-Mycenean era, a time of active and extensive trade between Greece, Crete, and the Near East, and the beginning of the Archaic period with its commercial and cultural expansion. Of these two, the earlier occasion seems far more likely.

Near Eastern Theogonies

The two most frequently cited examples of non-Greek influence on the Greek theogonic tradition as it is found in Hesiod's poem are the Akkadian-Babylonian creation epic, the "Enuma Elish," and the Hurrian-Hittite "Kingship in Heaven" (with its sequel, the "Song of Ullikummi").

The "Enuma Elish" (named for the first two words of the poem) is a ritual text which was recited annually to the god Marduk on the fourth day of the New Year's festival. Although no texts written earlier than the end of the 2nd millennium are known, the epic was once generally regarded as having been composed during the Amorite or Old Babylonian dynasty (19th-17th centuries), the age of the famous lawgiver Hammurabi. More recent opinion, however, has tended to reject this early dating and to place the composition of the epic during the Kassite period (the four centuries following the Old Babylonian period) or even later. Precise dating is not as important in regard to possible influence on Greece as some have thought; even if a late date is correct, the epic is based on earlier Akkadian and Sumerian material, and presumably the theogonic material at the beginning of the poem would be oldest and least resistant to change, as opposed to the detailed accounts of Marduk's new dispensation. The epic is written in the Akkadian dialect and, like most Babylonian mythological texts, is greatly dependent on Sumerian myths.

The Sumerians, whose language was neither Indo-European nor Semitic, were the first great civilization of Mesopotamia. They dominated the area throughout the third millennium, except for two centuries (about 2340-2150) during which Mesopotamia was ruled by the Semitic kingdom founded by the legendary Sargon, king of Akkad. The Sumerians regained dominance during the Third Dynasty of Ur (2125-2000), but disappeared as a separate people after another defeat by Semitic armies. The Sumerian language was no longer spoken, but continued to be written as an official language of some religious, political, and literary documents. Sumerian achievements in religion, literature, architecture, law, astronomy, and economic organization were adopted by succeeding Semitic peoples, and Sumerian culture remained the leading influence on the civilizations of Mesopotamia. When the Old Babylonian empire, perhaps under Hammurabi himself, set out to validate its rule and that of their god Marduk, the Sumerian creation myth was rewritten to make Marduk the ultimate ruler of all the gods and the "Enuma Elish," or an earlier version, was composed.

The "Enuma Elish" (*ANET* 60-72) begins with the union of primal waters, Apsu and Mummu-Tiamat; Apsu is male fresh waters and Tiamat is female sea waters (the epithet Mummu probably means "mother"). Within their waters are born the first gods: Lahmu and Lahamu, then Anshar and Kishar, then their son Anu (Sky) and Anu's son Ea, chief of the gods. The new gods disturb Apsu and Tiamat by their "loathsome" and "unsavory" behavior within the body of Tiamat, and Apsu decides to destroy the gods. Tiamat protests, but Apsu persists with his plan. Then Ea, the "all-wise," learns of Apsu's intention, casts a spell upon him, and kills him. Ea now marries Damkina and their son is Marduk, a giant with four eyes and four ears.

Some of the gods now complain to Tiamat about Marduk and persuade her to avenge Apsu. With the help of "Mother Hubur" (perhaps the earth goddess), who produces eleven monstrous children, Tiamat appoints Kingu, one of the "older gods," as commander, gives him the "Tablet of Destinies," and prepares for battle. Ea goes to Anshar for help and Anshar sends Anu to confront Tiamat, but Anu (like Ea before him) turns back in fear. Anshar then sends for Marduk, who agrees to fight Tiamat if the assembled gods proclaim him as supreme ruler. They grant Marduk his wish and, armed with a bow, mace, lightning, a net, eleven winds, and a storm-chariot, he goes to face Tiamat. At first sight of the "inside of Tiamat" and "Kingu, her consort," Marduk and his followers are temporarily confused and alarmed, but he quickly recovers and engages Tiamat in single combat; first, however, he accuses her of having caused a situation in which "sons reject their own fathers," of having given to Kingu the rightful position of Anu, of plotting evil against Anshar, and of not loving those whom she should.

In the combat Marduk snares Tiamat in his net; when she opens her mouth to swallow him, he sends in winds to hold her mouth open and her stomach distended, then shoots in an arrow and kills her. All her helpers, including Kingu and the monsters, are captured and imprisoned, and Marduk cuts Tiamat's body in half to create the sky and the earth. He then gives to the great gods (Anu, Ea, and Enlil) their proper places, arranges the weather and the heavenly bodies, and creates the features of the earth from parts of Tiamat's body. Finally Ea creates mankind from the blood of the rebel Kingu, for the express purpose of serving the gods. The epic ends with the building of a great temple in Babylon for Marduk, where a banquet is held at which the grateful gods recite the fifty honorific names of Marduk.

There are clear similarities between the Babylonian and Greek theogonies, and there are also many differences. Both begin with a primal couple (Apsu and Tiamat / Ouranos and Gaia) from whom the other gods are descended; children remain within the body of the first mother and are hated by their father; a solution is found by a clever god (Ea / Kronos) who defeats the father; the son (Marduk, who replaces Sumerian Enlil / Zeus) of the clever god then becomes king, but first must defeat monstrous enemies (the older gods and the monsters produced by Hubur, who seems functionally equivalent to Gaia and Rhea / the Titans, the Giants, and Typhoeus, all of whom are children of Gaia); mankind is created either by the clever god or during his reign.

Differences between the two epics, however, are more obvious than similarities, as a few examples will show. The first Babylonian couple are both water-gods, while the first Greek couple are Earth and Sky; the clever god Ea overthrows Apsu, not his father Sky, while Kronos overthrows his father Sky–in fact, the Babylonian Sky and his son, Anu and Ea, are allies against their common enemy Apsu; likewise Zeus overthrows his father Kronos and Kronos' brothers, while Marduk succeeds his great-grandfather Anshar, who is called "king of the gods," and defeats neither his father Ea nor Anshar, but is their champion against Tiamat.

It is unnecessary to extend the comparison, since it is clear that both myths share the same very general pattern, and that there is not much correspondence in details, especially the family relationships of characters to one another. Another recently-discovered Babylonian theogony (*ANET* 517-518) also displays a pattern similar to the Greek succession myth, but with characters different from either Hesiod or the "Enuma Elish." In it the first couple are Hain and Earth; Earth commands her son Amakandu to marry her, which he does and kills his father Hain; Amakandu then marries his sister Sea and their son Lahar kills his father and marries his mother; the unnamed son of Lahar and Sea kills both his parents and marries his sister River; their son kills his parents and marries his sister Ga'um; their son kills his parents and marries his sister Ningeshtinna; at this point the tablet becomes unreadable, although the same cyclic pattern of violence and incest seems to continue. While this theogony can hardly be a model for the Hesiodic version, it is nonetheless closer to it than the "Enuma Elish" in its insistence on father-son conflict and incest (both mother-son and brother-sister) as primary motives. On the other hand, incest is found (and is often logically necessary) in creation myths from around the world; this is especially true of the earliest cosmogonic myths of India, although it should be remembered that Hindu myth is Indo-European and therefore shares a common background with Greek myth.

Whatever the date of the "Enuma Elish" may be, it is probably best to say that it represents a common theogonic pattern in the Near East during the 2nd millennium which regularly was subject to local adaptation (as Marduk could replace Enlil, his Sumerian equivalent, or the Assyrian god Ashur could replace Marduk), and that the Greeks could have learned of this pattern at any time, the most probable guess being during the Minoan-Mycenean era.

Our second major example of possible Near Eastern influence on the Greek theogonic tradition is the Hurrian-Hittite "Kingship in Heaven" and "Song of Ullikummi," regarded by many scholars as the closest Near Eastern parallel to Hesiod. The Hurrians were a non-Indo-European, non-Semitic people (as were also the Sumerians) who moved south into Assyria at the beginning of the 2nd millennium and eventually migrated across northern Mesopotamia into Syria. They adopted many aspects of Mesopotamian culture, and it may be through Hurrian versions for the most part that the Greeks came to know Sumerian and Babylonian myths. The Hittites were an Indo-European tribe who appeared in Asia Minor about 1800; by the 14th century they had won control of Syria, and during the New Kingdom (about 1450-1200) they were one of the great powers of the Near East. The Hittites were approximate contemporaries of the Myceneans, and their two languages are our earliest examples of a written Indo-European language (in both cases in a borrowed script–the Myceneans used the Minoan syllabary and the Hittites used the Babylonian cuneiform). Some of the more than 10,000 texts found at the Hittite capital Hattusas are mythological and religious, and most of these are Hittite versions of Hurrian myths, which had themselves been influenced by Mesopotamian precedents.

"Kingship in Heaven" (*ANET* 120-121) begins with the reign of Alalu in heaven; after nine years, he is overthrown by Anu (Sky) and goes down to the "dark earth;" Anu rules for nine years and then is attacked by Kumarbi and flees to the sky; Kumarbi pursues, seizes Anu by the feet, and then bites off and swallows Anu's genitals; when Kumarbi begins to laugh, Anu tells him that because of what he has swallowed he is now pregnant with three gods: the Storm-God Heshub (the chief god of the Hurrians and Hittites), the river Aranzaha (the Tigris), and Tasmisu (an attendant of the Storm-God); Anu now hides in the sky and Kumarbi spits out what he can (later Aranzaha and Tasmisu will be born from the earth), but the Storm-God remains inside him; Anu now speaks to the Storm-God and the two have a long debate about how the Storm-God should escape from Kumarbi's body; Kumarbi becomes dizzy and asks Aya (Ea) for something to eat; he eats something (variously read as "stone" or "son"), but it hurts his mouth; finally the Storm-God, after being warned not to exit through other orifices, especially the anus, comes out through Kumarbi's "good place," evidently his penis; at this point the text becomes unreadable, but the Storm-God must defeat Kumarbi and become king.

In the "Song of Ullikummi" (*ANET* 121-125) Kumarbi plots revenge; he has intercourse repeatedly with a huge female rock, who gives birth to a stone child, Ullikummi; the child is hidden from the Storm-God and placed on the right shoulder of Ubelluri (the Hurrian Atlas), where he grows at the rate of an acre per month; the first battle between the Storm-God and Ullikummi, who is now 9,000 leagues high, ends with the Storm-God's defeat; the gods are upset and threatened by Ullikummi, and Ea orders the "old gods" to bring out the ancient copper "cutter" with which heaven and earth had been separated, and to use this to cut through the feet of Ullikummi; the Storm-God again comes to fight Ullikummi (and must defeat him, although the final lines cannot be read).

The parallels between the Hurrian and Hesiodic myths are clear once we eliminate the reign of Alalu: Anu is equivalent to Ouranos, Kumarbi to Kronos, and the Storm-God to Zeus; Anu and Ouranos are both castrated and various gods are born from their severed genitals; Kumarbi and Kronos castrate their fathers and have children inside themselves; the Storm-God and Zeus win the kingship of the gods, then must win a second victory over an enormous monster (Ullikummi/Typhoeus).

The parallels cannot be pressed too far. For example, is the Storm-God the son of Kumarbi, from whom he is born, or of Anu, whose genitals make Kumarbi pregnant, or of both, with Anu as father and Kumarbi as mother? Also, Zeus, unlike the Storm-God, never shares his siblings' fate of being inside Kronos but is rescued by the trickery of Rhea and Gaia. As for the similarity between the monsters Ullikummi and Typhoeus, the Hurrian myth seems closer to the much later version of Apollodoros (1.6.3) than to Hesiod's (but according to Apollodoros it is Zeus, not the monster, whose feet are cut through).

The most probable estimate of the relationship between the Hurrian myth and the *Theogony* is that neither version directly influenced the other, but that both go back to some common Mesopotamian source. Where the Babylonian "Enuma Elish" would appear in this line of derivation would depend on its early or late dating, and in any case is not as important as the recognition that the Greek *Theogony* occupies a relatively late position in a complex, widespread, and interrelated theogonic tradition encompassing western Asia and the Mediterranean.

Hesiod's Theogony°

Let us begin to sing of the Muses of Helikon,°
who hold the great and holy mount of Helikon,°
and dance on tender feet round the violet spring
and the altar° of Kronos' mighty son.
Having washed their soft skin in Permessos'°   5
spring, or Hippokrene, or holy Olmeios,
on Helikon's summit° they lead the fair and
beautiful dances with rapid steps.
Setting out from there, concealed by air,
they walk at night, chanting their fair song,   10

Title We do not know what name (if any) Hesiod gave to his poem; the generic term
theogonia is certainly appropriate, and the poem may have been identified simply
as "a theogony." Our earliest evidence for the use of *Theogony* as a specific title
occurs in the fragments of the Stoic philosopher Chrysippos, five centuries after
Hesiod.

1 The Muses invoked by Hesiod are the divine patronesses of song and singers. It was
a common practice in early Greek poetry to begin a recitation with an appeal to
them (or to one of them) for inspiration and guidance. The first line of the *Iliad* ad-
dresses a Muse as "goddess" and the first line of the *Odyssey* calls upon an anonymous "Muse," as do *Hh* 4, 5, 9, 14, 17, 19, and 20; *Hh* 25, 32, and 33 address the
Muses as a group, and 31 specifically invokes the Muse Kalliope. It was also usual
for early singers to begin their performance with a hymn to a god or gods as an introduction; the shorter *Hymns* are clearly prefaces of this sort. Hesiod introduces
his song with a hymn to the Muses because they are more than a poetic convention
to him; they actually appeared to him and made him a singer (22-33), and they
commanded him to sing first of themselves.

2 Mount Helikon is the highest mountain of Boiotia, about halfway between Thebes
and Delphi. The town of Askra on its slopes was the home of Hesiod; according to
Pausanias (9.29.1-2) Askra was founded by the Aloadai (two gigantic children who
tried to take over Olympos), and they also started a cult of the Muses on Helikon.

4 There may have been a cult of Zeus on Helikon, as the presence of an altar implies.

5-6 The Permessos is a stream of Helikon, and the Olmeios is a nearby river into
which it flowed. Hippokrene, a spring high on Helikon, was later said to have been
created by a kick of the hoof of the winged horse Pegasos; the name means "spring
of the horse."

7-10 The Muses are coming down from Helikon's summit because they are on their
way to meet Hesiod, as described in 22-34.

singing° of Zeus Aigiochos° and mistress Hera
of Argos,° who walks in golden sandals, and
Zeus Aigiochos' daughter, owl-eyed Athena,
and Phoibos Apollo and archeress Artemis,
and Poseidon earth-embracer,° earth-shaker,   15
and revered Themis° and glancing Aphrodite,
and gold-crowned Hebe and lovely Dione,°
Leto, Iapetos,° and crafty Kronos,
Eos, great Helios, and bright Selene,°
Gaia, great Okeanos, and black Nyx,° and   20

11-21 Like Hesiod, the Muses sing of gods and goddesses, and all of the deities named here will appear later in the *Theogony*, although not in this order.

11 Zeus' descriptive epithet "Aigiochos" is usually translated "aegis-bearing" and thought to refer to the *aigis*, a goat-skin emblem made by Hephaistos for Zeus, who uses it to frighten enemies and create thunder-storms. But West (*WD* 366-368) has shown that for linguistic reasons the epithet probably refers to a goat (aix) and not an *aigis*, and should mean "riding on a goat" or "being drawn by a goat." Furthermore, aix means not only "goat" but also a kind of bird which may be a snipe, and the snipe is associated in several European cultures with storms or a storm-god. Thus, just as Athena is "owl-eyed" and Hera is "cow-eyed," Zeus is "goat (or snipe)-drawn."

12 Hera's epithet *Argeia* reflects the ancient worship of Hera at Argos, where she was the goddess of the city (as Athena was at Athens).

15 Poseidon is called "earth-embracer" because he is a sea-god, and the ocean was regarded by the gods as a circular river which surrounded the earth; a similar meaning may be present in the etymology of Poseidon's name, which could mean "husband of earth."

16 Themis is a Titan goddess (135) and Zeus' second wife (901).

17 Hebe [Youth] is a daughter of Zeus and Hera (922). Dione is an Okeanid nymph in the *Theogony* (353), but Homer and some other sources call her the mother of Aphrodite; her name is a feminine form of "Zeus."

18 Leto is a daughter of the Titans Koios and Phoibe (404-406) and Zeus' sixth wife (918); their children are Apollo and Artemis (919). Iapetos is a Titan (134) and the father of Prometheus (510).

19 Eos [Dawn], Helios [Sun], and Selene [Moon] are children of the Titans Theia and Hyperion (371-374).

20 Gaia [Earth], Okeanos, and Nyx [Night] may all have played important roles in variant theogonic traditions known to Hesiod. Gaia is the primal parent of the *Theogony*, but the possibility that Okeanos had a similar function in another theogony is suggested by references in the *Iliad* (14.201, 14.246) to Okeanos as the source of all the gods. There may have been a tradition in which Okeanos and his wife Tethys were the first parents, just as the water-gods Tiamat and Apsu are the first couple in the "Enuma Elish" (*In* 22). Or perhaps there was a version in which Okeanos and Gaia, water and earth, were the first parents (*Ps* 94); the early mythographer Pherekydes speaks of a union between Okeanos and Gaia, and Hesiod mentions a union between Gaia and the sea-god Pontos, her son and Okeanos' half-

the holy race of other immortals who always are.
Once they taught Hesiod beautiful song°
as he watched his sheep° under holy Helikon;
this is the first thing the goddesses told me,
the Olympian Muses,° daughters of Zeus Aigiochos: 25
   "Rustic shepherds, evil oafs, nothing but bellies,°
we know how to say many lies as if they were true,°
and when we want, we know how to speak the truth."
   This is what the prompt-voiced daughters of great Zeus said;
they picked and gave me a staff, a branch of strong laurel,°   30

---

brother (131-132). Nyx appears as the first being or as one of the first pairs of beings in the early cosmogonies attributed to Mousaios and Epimenides, as well as one of the Orphic versions, and in her dark obscurity is similar to Chaos, Hesiod's first being.

22 We may presume that the Muses did not actually appear to Hesiod, but we may not presume that he did not think they did, in a dream, day-dream, or vision of some sort; gods have been appearing regularly to mortals since religion began. On the other hand, this kind of divine visitation may have already become a poetic convention by the time of Hesiod; he may be saying "the Muses made me a singer" in the same way we say "the devil made me do it."

23 The sheep watched by Hesiod may also be a poetic convention (West, *T* 160).

25 The "Olympian" Muses are the same as the "Helikonian" Muses in 1; they are called Helikonian because Helikon is one of their favorite places and a site of their cult, and Olympian because they sing to and of their father Zeus, whose home is Olympos. G. Nagy ("Hesiod" in *Great Writers: Greece and Rome*, ed. T. J. Luce, Vol. 1 [New York, 1982] 55-56) has suggested that the distinction between Helikonian and Olympian is the difference between local variant theogonies and the Hesiodic panhellenic theogony which superseded them.

26 The colloquial insults with which the Muses address Hesiod are 1) a convention in primitive and archaic ritual; 2) a convention in visions of superior gods to inferior mortals (West, *T* 160), and 3) because they are addressed to a plural audience, a characterization of a class of people (ignorant farmers) among whom Hesiod will be an exception, precisely because of the Muses' favor.

27-28 The lies which have the appearance of truth may refer to variants and contradictions in the theogonic traditions which Hesiod knew. They may once have seemed true and may still seem so to some people, but Hesiod now will learn and sing the truth about such matters, thanks to the guidance of the Muses.

30 To hold a staff, in early Greek literature, is to have the authority to speak; staffs are held by kings, priests, prophets, heralds, and speakers in the Homeric assembly of chieftains. Professional singers after the time of Hesiod often carried a laurel wand, and an ancient commentator claimed that Hesiod invented this practice (no doubt using this passage as his evidence). The laurel is associated with Apollo and with oracles and prophecy; it is therefore fitting for singers also, since singers and prophets in ancient Greece shared a calling and knowledge not available to ordinary mortals. There were other concrete signs (blindness, for example) which, at least in myth and legend, characterize both singers and prophets as possessors of arcane knowledge.

a fine one, and breathed into me a voice°
divine, to celebrate what will be and what was.
They told me to sing the race of the blessed who always are,
but always to sing of themselves first and also last.
But what is this of oak or rock to me?°   35
      Hesiod, let us start from the Muses, who with singing°
cheer the great mind of father Zeus in Olympos,°   *Zeus is the God.*
telling things that are and will be and were before, *—*
with harmonized voice; the unbroken song flows
sweet from their lips; the father's house rejoices,   40
the house of loud-sounding° Zeus, as the delicate voice
Of the goddesses spreads, the peaks of snowy Olympos echo,
and the homes of the immortals; with ambrosial voice
they praise in song° first the august race of gods
from the beginning, whom Gaia and wide Ouranos begot,   45
and those born from them, the gods, givers of good;
and second of Zeus, the father of gods and men, *— father figure*
[the goddesses sing, beginning and ending the song]
how he is best of gods and greatest in power;
next, singing of the race of men and mighty Giants°   50
they cheer the mind of Zeus in Olympos, themselves

31-32 As a result of the Muses' inspiration, Hesiod will sing of "what will be and what
was." Knowledge of both past and future is another characteristic shared by mythical singers and prophets.

35 This puzzling line must be a proverb of some kind. Ancient evidence and modern
interpretations are discussed in detail by West (*T* 167-169), who admits that "the
truth is lost in antiquity." The meaning may be "Why do I speak further of incred-
ible things?" (i.e., the epiphany of the Muses), but this cannot be demonstrated. At
any rate, the verse is an indication that one topic is ending and another is about to
begin.

36-103 Having told of his own relationship with the Muses, Hesiod now starts over.
This second part of his prologue is much more like the standard hymn to a divinity,
relating the Muses' function and situation among the gods (37-74), the details of
their parentage and birth (53-62), their names (75-79), and their functions in regard
to mortals (80-103).

37 The chief function of the Muses is to entertain Zeus; they sing to cheer his mind
(37, 51), and their song is mostly about him (47, 49, 53-54, 56-67, 71-74).

41 Zeus is "loud-sounding" because he is a thunder-, lightning-, and storm-god.

44-50 The song of the Muses recapitulates the themes of the *Theogony* and its sequel,
the *Catalogue of Women*: the first gods and the Titans (44-45), the Olympian gods
(46), Zeus (47, 49), mortals 50).

50 Why the Muses sing of mortals and Giants together is puzzling, especially since the
battle of Zeus with the Giants is not mentioned in the *Theogony*, which tells only of
the Giants' conception and birth (185-186). Herakles, while still a mortal, was the

the Muses of Olympos, daughters of Zeus Aigiochos.
Mnemosyne, who rules the hills of Eleuther,° having lain
with the father, Kronos' son, in Pieria,° bore them to be
a forgetting of evils and a respite from cares.°   55
For wise Zeus lay with her nine nights°
apart from the immortals, going up to the holy bed;
but when a year went by, and the seasons turned round,
as moons waned, and many days were completed,
she bore nine like-minded daughters, in whose   60
breasts and spirit song is the only care,
just below the summit of snowy Olympos. There
are their polished dance-floors and lovely houses;
next to them the Charites and Himeros have homes°
in joy; chanting from their lips a sweet song,   65
they sing, and praise the customs and noble ways of
all the immortals, chanting a most sweet song.
Then they went to Olympos, rapt in the lovely air,°
the ambrosial song; the black earth echoed round
to their singing, and a sweet beat arose under their   70
feet as they went to their father; he was ruling the
sky, holding the thunder and fiery lightning-bolt himself,
having conquered father Kronos by might; in right detail
he dealt laws and appointed honors to the immortals.

---

indispensable participant in the gods' battle against the Giants (*Ap* 1.6.1), and this
may be hinted at in 954, but 954 was probably not written by Hesiod and there is
no clear reference to this battle in literature or art until a century after Hesiod.

53 Mnemosyne, the mother of the Muses, is the personification of Memory, and therefore most important to a poet whose tradition is entirely or largely orally transmit-
ted. Eleuther is on Mount Kithairon, another Boiotian mountain which may have
been the site of a cult of the Muses, as well as the place where the infant Oidipous
was exposed and where Herakles killed a monstrous lion.

54 Pieria, the area north of Mount Olympos in Thessaly, was well-known in antiquity
for its cult of the Muses.

55 That Memory should bear "forgetfulness" is an oxymoron and almost a pun.

56-60 The intercourse of Zeus and Mnemosyne lasts for nine nights because she will
bear nine children. Somewhat similarly, Zeus is said to have enjoyed the night he
spent with Alkmene so much that he extended the night to three times its normal
length (*Ap* 2.4.8), and this inordinate amount of time was responsible for the great
strength of Herakles, the child Alkmene conceived (Diodoros 4.9).

64 The Charites [Graces] are three daughters of Zeus and Eurynome (907-909).
Himeros [Longing] is an attendant of Aphrodite (201), but his parentage is not
given in early Greek literature.

68 The Muses' procession to Olympos presumably follows immediately after their
birth.

These things the Muses sang, who hold Olympian homes,°   75
nine daughters begotten by great Zeus,
Kleio, Euterpe, Thaleia, and Melpomene,
Terpsichore, Erato, Polymnia, Ourania,
and Kalliope, who is most eminent of all,
for she is companion of reverent kings.°   80
Whomever of kings, favored by Zeus, the daughters
of great Zeus honor and see being born,
they pour sweet dew on his tongue, and
from his lips flow honeyed words; his people
all look to him as he decides issues with   85
straight judgments; speaking unerringly he
quickly and wisely ends even great strife;
this is why there are sensible kings, since
they secure restitution for the wronged in
public and easily, persuading by soft words;   90
going to assembly, they pray to him as to a god,
with supplicant awe; in assembly he is pre-eminent.
Such is the holy gift of the Muses to men.
For from the Muses and far-shooting Apollo
are men on earth who sing and play the harp,   95
but kings are from Zeus; he prospers, whom the
Muses love; a sweet voice flows from his lips.
For if one has grief in his newly-vexed spirit,° and

75-79 The number and names of the nine Muses may have been invented by Hesiod.
There is of course no way to prove this, but a reason to suspect that the names oc-
cur here for the first time is the fact that the names reflect words and phrases earlier
used by Hesiod (West, *T* 180-181). For example, Kleio appears in *kleiousin* (67),
Erato in *eraten* (65) and *eratos* (70), Kalliope in *opi kale* (68). It was not until late
Roman times that individual Muses were given separate authority for different arts:
Kleio for history, Euterpe for music, Thaleia for comedy, Melpomene for tragedy,
Terpsichore for dance, Erato for lyric poetry, Polymnia for mime, Ourania for astronomy, and Kalliope for epic poetry (there were many variations of this list). A
modern "museum" is a "place of the Muses" [*mouseion*], and in ancient Greece
philosophers (such as Plato and Aristotle) and scholars put their schools under the
sponsorship of the Muses.

80-97 The Muses have functions among mortals as well as among the gods, and kings
are an obvious example of the benefit of their assistance. If rulers are not to rely on
force on every occasion, they must be able to persuade their subjects with inspired
words. Also, the *Theogony* may have been composed for a competition at Chalkis
in honor of a dead king and before a royal audience (*In* 2); it would not hurt Hesiod's prospects if he inserted his judges in his poem.

98-103 Mention of a "newly-vexed spirit" whose "grief" is diverted by a singer also
suggests that Hesiod's poem is intended for performance at a funeral (West, *T* 45).

his heart is withered in sorrow, and then a bard,
the Muses' servant, sings the fame of former men   100
and the blessed gods who hold Olympos, soon
he forgets his mind's burden and remembers none of
his cares; quickly the goddesses' gifts divert him.
    Greetings, children of Zeus; grant me lovely song,°
and praise the holy race of immortals who always are,   105
who were born from Gaia and starry Ouranos,°
and from dark Nyx, and those salty Pontos raised.
Tell how at first gods and earth came to be,
and rivers and vast sea, violent in surge,
and shining stars and the wide sky above,   110
[and the gods born from them, givers of good]
how they divided their wealth and allotted honors _ *like brothers sharing*
and how first they held valed Olympos.   *fathers things.*
Tell me these things, Muses with Olympian homes,
from the first, say which of them first came to be.°   115
    First° of all Chaos° came into being; but next
wide-breasted Gaia, always safe foundation of all

104-115 Again Hesiod seems to start over. This section describes the main genealogical concerns of his poem, and also suggests his main purpose, to depict the establishment of a permanent divine hierarchy on Olympos (112-113).

106-107 The descendants of Gaia and Ouranos will include not only the Titans, their
children, but ultimately all the Olympian gods and goddesses (and a great many
others). The children of Nyx are the fifteen singular and collective personifications
named in 211-225, and the children of Pontos are Nereus (233), father of the
Nereid nymphs (240-264), and four others (237-239) from whom most mythical
monsters will be descended (265-336).

115-116 The last line of the prologue leads directly into the main body of the poem.
Hesiod asks the Muses to say what "first came to be" [*proton genet'*] and the
Muses' answer follows immediately: "first of all Chaos came into being" [*protista
Chaos genet'*]. The remainder of the *Theogony* is the song the Muses taught to He-
siod.

116-122 The world begins with a stage radically set apart from everything that follows, in that the first four beings to appear are spontaneously generated without
source or cause (*Ps* 90-93).

116 The primary meaning of the Greek word *chaos* is not disorder or confusion, but
rather an opening or gap. Related to the verb *chasko* [open, yawn, gape], *chaos* signifies a void, an abyss, infinite space and darkness, unformed matter. The etymology may suggest a womb which opens to bring forth life, but there are much
stronger connotations of an impenetrable and immeasurable darkness, an opacity in
which order is non-existent or at least unperceived. The concept of a primordial
Chaos is reminiscent of the boundless and featureless watery waste called Nun in
Egyptian cosmogony and the formless void and abyss of *Genesis*.

immortals who possess the peaks of snowy Olympos,°
and dim Tartaros° in a recess of the wide-pathed earth,
and Eros,° most beautiful among the immortal gods,   120
limb-weakener, who conquers the mind and sensible thought
in the breasts of all gods and all men.
    From Chaos were born Erebos and black Nyx;°
from Nyx were born Aither and Hemera,

117-118 Gaia is not only the earth, but also the primal mother from whom almost all
of subsequent creation is descended. In virtually all cosmogonies (with the topog-
raphically determined exception of the Egyptian) Earth is the primordial maternal
symbol, and in Greek myth she plays an especially important role as mother and
wife of Ouranos, mother of the Titans, and grandmother of Zeus and the first generation of Olympian gods. There is a suggestion in *WD* 108 that mortals also were
born from Earth: "gods and mortal men are born from the same source." Hesiod
calls Earth "mother of all" (*WD* 563), and Euripides uses the same phrase in a fragment which also refers to the birth of men from the earth: "Earth, who receives the
wet rain-drops and bears mortals, bears plants and the tribe of beasts; therefore you
are rightly called mother of all". The connection between Earth and Mother was
felt so strongly by the Greeks that Plato could say "The woman in her conception
and generation is but the imitation of the earth, and not the earth of the woman"
(*Menexenus* 238a).

119 Tartaros is the lowest part of the underworld, and since the underworld is everything below the surface of the earth, Tartaros seems to be the lowest part of Earth.
Like many cosmogonic phenomena, Tartaros is both a place and also a (barely) anthropomorphized being, who mates and produces offspring but has no personality
or career. Tartaros is not mentioned in the *Odyssey*, but is described in *Iliad* 8.13-
16 in terms quite similar to Hesiod's description at 720-725. In early Greek literature the underworld is usually called the "house of Hades (and/or Persephone)";
later (and once in Homer, *Iliad* 23.244) "home of" tends to be omitted, and the
place as well as the god who rules it are called simply "Hades." The Titans and the
monster Typhoeus are specifically mentioned as being thrown into Tartaros by
Zeus (717-731, 868), and Tartaros may be the "dark hole" of Earth in which Ouranos confines his children (158); the Greek word for "dark hole" is *keuthmon*, and
Aeschylus will later speak of the *keuthmon* of Tartaros (*Prometheus* 222). In later
Greek literature Tartaros became the underworld home of a select group of criminals, the most famous and earliest being Tantalos, Sisyphos, Tityos, and Ixion (*Ps*
90-93).

120 Eros is a creative principle of Desire in the universe; his appearance is the necessary condition separating the first stage of the world from all later development.
After Eros comes into existence, all creation will be procreation (*Ps* 89).

123 First Chaos, and then Gaia (126-132), begin reproducing. The breadth of the Hesiodic concept of Eros is suggested by the fact that the first children to be produced
are fatherless: Erebos and Nyx are born to Chaos, and Ouranos, the Ourea, and
Pontos to Gaia. It is not until this point (133) that Eros is sexualized and becomes
desire of a reproductive partner. The darkness of Chaos is replicated in her children
Erebos [Darkness] and "black Nyx" [Night].

whom she conceived and bore, joined in love with Erebos.°   125
Gaia first bore a child° equal to herself,
starry Ouranos, to cover her all over, and
to be an always safe home for the blessed gods.
She bore the high Ourea,° pleasing homes of divine
Nymphs, who dwell in the valed mountains.   130
She also bore the barren sea,° violent in surge,
Pontos, without love's union; but next
she lay with Ouranos° and bore deep-whirling Okeanos,

124-125 The union of Darkness and Night produces Aither [Brightness] and Hemera [Day], their elemental and complementary opposites.

126-128 Gaia's first child Ouranos [Sky] is also her complement; the phrases "equal to herself" and "to cover her all over" seem to depict Earth and Sky as two halves of one large mass. This would correspond well with the hypothesis that Earth and Sky are engaged in continual intercourse (see on 154-160), and appears in mythical form in a fragment of Euripides: "Earth and Sky were one shape, and when they were separated they begot all things."

129-130 The Ourea are the Mountains, and the nymphs who dwell in them are often called Oread nymphs (*ourea* is a poetic form of *orea*).

131-132 Gaia's final parthenogenic son is Pontos [Sea], by whom she will later produce children (233-239). The distinction between Pontos and Okeanos, Sea and Ocean, is based on the identification of Okeanos as a river which encircled the earth.

133 The marriage of Gaia and her son Ouranos, Earth and Sky, is found in many cosmogonies around the world. The interesting and obvious question about their relationshp is how Sky above and Earth below manage to connect with one another in order to produce children. A completely anthropomorphized answer would see them as two huge bodies lying one on top of the other, a notion which seems required by Hesiod's story of the castration of Ouranos. The usual answer, however, is metaphoric rather than anthropomorphic, and views this cosmic sexuality in the form of rain and lightning, projections of the sky-god's procreative power (*Ps* 94-95); the fragment from Aeschylus' *Danaides* cited there reads: "Eros makes holy Ouranos lie with Gaia, Eros makes Gaia want to lie with Ouranos; rain falling from Ouranos' coming makes Gaia pregnant. She bears flocks of sheep, and grain, so men may live; the forest comes to life, watered by this marriage." Ouranos is the Indo-European father-sky-god, of whom Zeus will be the third, last, and greatest version. Although the first Indo-Europeans to enter Greece presumably brought with them an earth-goddess mate for their sky-god, she must have soon been assimilated with the great mother-earth-goddess who dominated the Mediterranean religions the first Greeks encountered. The clearest example of such assimilation between the two cultures appears in the myth of Zeus' birth on the island of Crete (477-484). The circular river Okeanos is the eldest child of Gaia and Ouranos and the father of 6000 other rivers and Okeanid nymphs (337-370). He seems rather out of place in the list of Titans, and this may be due to the possibility that Hesiod transplanted him here from another version in which his role was that of a primal parent (see on 20).

and Koios and Kreios and Hyperion and Iapetos,
and Theia and Rhea and Themis and Mnemosyne   135
and gold-crowned Phoibe and attractive Tethys.
After them was born the youngest, crafty Kronos,°
most terrible of children; he hated his lusting father.°

Next she bore the Kyklopes° with over-proud heart,
Brontes and Steropes and hard-hearted Arges,   140
who gave Zeus thunder and made the lightning-bolt.
They were like the gods in everything else,
but a single eye was in the middle of their foreheads;
they were given the name Kyklopes because
one round eye was in their foreheads;   145
strength, force, and skill were in their works.
Next others were born from Gaia and Ouranos,
three great and mighty sons, unspeakable

133-137 The twelve children here named will be called the Titans by their father Ouranos in 207. It was once thought that the Titans represented the gods of the pre-
Greek indigenous population of Greece, but our present knowledge of Near Eastern
parallels suggests that the concept of a group of gigantic older gods (e.g., Kingu
and the "older gods" in the "Enuma Elish") was borrowed from the East, perhaps
during the Mycenean period. Koios, Kreios, and Hyperion have virtually no separate identities and serve only a genealogical function (Koios is father of Leto and
Hyperion of Helios). The same is true of Phoibe and Theia, the wives of Koios and
Hyperion. Kreios' wife will be the almost equally colorless Eurybia, daughter of
Gaia and Pontos, who is at least distinguished by having a "heart of adamant"
(239). Themis and Mnemosyne will become wives of Zeus (901, 915), Tethys is
the wife of Okeanos (and, like him, perhaps one of the primal couple in a variant
theogony), and Iapetos (whose name resembles that of Noah's son Japheth in
Genesis) will be the father of Prometheus and his brothers (507-511). Besides
Okeanos, the only Titans to have much of a story connected with them are Kronos
and Rhea, who succeed Ouranos and Gaia as the ruling couple.

138 The reasons why Kronos is "most terrible" and why he "hated his lusting father"
will be revealed in 156-181. Kronos' chronological position as youngest son prede-
termines his eventual succession to his father's throne (*Ps* 95-96).

139-146 The names of the Kyklopes-Brontes, Steropes, Arges-mean Thunderer, Light-
ner, and Flashing. These Kyklopes, who make the lightning-bolts which are Zeus'
chief weapon, are sometimes called the "ouranian" Kyklopes for their father Ouranos; later Hephaistos will replace them as armorer of the gods, with the Kyklopes
as his assistants. Already in the *Odyssey* there is a second group of Kyklopes, a
primitive race of giants met by Odysseus either in Sicily or on the coast of Italy.
The Greeks also believed that a race of Kyklopes built the fortification walls whose
ruins they observed on Mycenean sites (*In* 19); these Kyklopes were supposed to
have helped Proitos fortify Tiryns and Perseus fortify Argos. The single great eye
and huge size of the Kyklopes, as well as their place in the older generation of
gods, may reflect the strongest impression received by an infant's immature vision
of an adult face a few inches away.

Kottos and Briareos and Gyges, rash children.
From their shoulders shot a hundred arms   150
unimaginable, and fifty heads on the shoulders
of each grew over their strong bodies;
great and mighty strength was in their huge shape.°
　　For all° who were born from Gaia and Ouranos were the
most terrible of children, and their father hated them   155
from the first; when any of them first would be born,
he would hide them all away, and not let them come up
to the light, in a dark hole of Gaia; the evil deed
pleased Ouranos. But she, vast Gaia, groaned within
from the strain, and planned an evil crafty trick.   160
Quick she made the element of grey adamant,°
made a great sickle,° and advised her sons,
speaking encouragingly, while hurt in her heart:°
　　"Children of me and a wicked father, if you are willing
to obey, we may punish the evil outrage of your   165
father; since he first planned unseemly deeds."
She said this,° but fear seized them all and none of them
spoke. But great and crafty Kronos was brave, and

[handwritten marginalia: — contrasting description of both odmiration, and hatred toward Kronos.]

147-153 The three Hundred-Handed, as later mythographers call them, do not have
　　names as explicitly metaphoric as those of the Kyklopes. Kottos seems to be a
　　Thracian name, Briareus has connotations of strength, and Gyges may be related to
　　Ogyges, a mythical Attic king (West, *T* 209-210). The name Ogyges became syn-
　　onymous with "primaeval"; the "primal water" of Styx (805) is "*hydor ogygion*."
154-160 All the children of Ouranos share Kronos' attribute of "most terrible," and the
　　reason for this, as well as the reason Kronos hated his father, is now made clear;
　　their father hates them and refuses to allow them to come out of the body of their
　　mother. Ouranos hates his children because he has married his mother, and he fears
　　that his children will want to follow his example and replace him (*In* 16). The "dark
　　hole" of Gaia in which the children are confined is presumably her womb, and this
　　innermost place of the earth may also be Tartaros. The means by which Ouranos
　　suppresses his children must be continuous sexual intercourse with Gaia; this
　　would explain why their imprisonment will be ended immediately by castration.
161 Adamant is a mythical element, hardest of all metals; it means "unconquerable."
162 A sickle is the weapon often used to fight monsters. Perseus uses a sickle to de-
　　capitate the Gorgon Medousa, and Iolaos uses a sickle to help Herakles against the
　　monstrous Hydra during Herakles' second labor. In various later versions the sickle
　　of Kronos was said to have been thrown into the sea; from it several places were
　　suipposed to have grown, such as Sicily, the Homeric island of the Phaiakians, and
　　Cape Drepanon in Greece.
163-175 How Gaia manages to speak to the children inside her should not present a
　　problem; in the Hurrian "Kingship in Heaven" myth, Anu has a long conversation
　　with Heshub, who is inside the body of Kumarbi. Kronos' place of "ambush" must
　　be a position closest to the surface of Earth.

quickly gave an answer to his dear mother:
  "Mother, I would undertake and do this task,   170
since I have no respect for our father
unspeakable; since he first planned unseemly deeds."
  He spoke and vast Gaia was greatly pleased in her mind.
She placed and hid him in ambush, and put in his hands
a sickle with jagged teeth, and revealed the whole trick.   175
Great Ouranos came, bringing on night,° and upon Gaia
he lay, wanting love and fully extended;
his son,° from ambush, reached out with his left hand
and with his right hand took the huge sickle,
long with jagged teeth, and quickly severed   180
his own father's genitals, and threw them to fall
behind; they did not fall from his hand without result,
for all the bloody drops which spurted were
received by Gaia; as the year revolved,

---

176 Sky's embrace of Earth is so close it blots out the light, thus "bringing on night."

178-187 The castration of Ouranos, which accomplishes the separation of Earth and Sky, is reminiscent of the castration of Anu [Sky] in "Kingship in Heaven." A further similarity is the fertility of castration: Kumarbi, who swallows the genitals of Anu, becomes pregnant with three gods, two of whom are born when Kumarbi spits out part of what he had swallowed on the earth; Kronos' severed genitals are transformed into Aphrodite and the drops of blood which fall on the earth produce three groups of offspring. The Erinyes are the Furies, mythical spirits of retributive vengeance who punish those crimes, especially within the family, which threaten the traditional structures of home and society. Their particular concern with the crimes of children against parents may be seen in their relentless pursuit of the mythical matricides Orestes and Alkmaion. Themselves born from the crime of sons against their father, the Erinyes are symbols of guilt, especially that attached to the enactment of hostile impulses against parents. Born from castration, they are themselves castrating, as Apollo reminds them in Aeschylus' *Eumenides* 185-190: "It is not fit that you inhabit this house, but rather where there are beheadings and eye-gougings and throat-slit judgments, and by castration the virility of young men is ruined, and mutilations and stoning, and men moan most pitiably, impaled under the spine." The names of the three Erinyes, according to *Ap* 1.1.4, are Alekto, Tisiphone, and Megaira. The Giants will have a long gestation period within the earth, since Gaia will keep them inside her until a time comes when she will need champions to fight for her. That occasion will occur when she decides to punish Zeus for his defeat of the Titans, her children; the resultant war between the Olympian gods and the Giants [the Gigantomachy] is a near-duplicate of the battle between Olympians and Titans [the Titanomachy] and is described most fully in *Ap* 1.6.1-2, although it was already a favorite subject for the sculpted decorations of temples by the 6th century. The nymphs called Meliai are properly "ash-tree" nymphs; the Greek word for ash-trees is *meliai* also. Why they are mentioned here, or born in this way, is unclear and may reflect a local aetiological myth.

she bore the strong Erinyes and great Giants,   185
shining in armor, holding long spears in their hands,
and the nymphs called Meliai on the endless earth.
As soon as he cut off the genitals with adamant,°
he threw them from land into the turbulent sea;
they were carried over the sea a long time, and white   190
foam arose from the immortal flesh; within a girl
grew; first she came to holy Kythera, and
next she came to wave-washed Cyprus.
An awesome and beautiful goddess emerged, and
grass grew under her supple feet. Aphrodite   195
[foam-born goddess and well-crowned Kythereia]
gods and men name her, since in foam she grew;
and Kythereia, since she landed at Kythera;
and Kyprogenes, since she was born in wave-beat Cyprus;
and "Philommeides,"° since she appeared from the genitals.   200
Eros accompanied her, and fair Himeros followed,°

188-199 The birth of Aphrodite from the castration of Ouranos is not so bizarre or at
least so incongruous as it may seem. Just as Athena, goddess of wisdom, will be
born from the head of Zeus, now the goddess of sexual desire is born from a god's
genitals. Furthermore, the appearance of a symbol of desire immediately after, and
as a result of, an act of castration repeats the pattern of 119-120, where the emergence of Tartaros, a place associated with castration, leads to the appearance of
Eros (*Ps* 91). Hesiod's Aphrodite, like Eros, is a primal erotic principle which
comes into existence at the world's beginning. The name of Aphrodite contains
aphros [foam] and is commonly interpreted to mean "born from foam." But this
would be *aphrogenes* (196) or something similar, and Hesiod says that she grew
within the foam, not from it; the severed penis of Ouranos is what is transformed
into the goddess, just as the genitals of Anu become the three gods of the Hurrian
myth. A possible explanation of the foam in both her name and the myth is that
sea-foam symbolizes semen, a possibility which occurs in several Greek sources
and in the Hindu epic *Mahabharata*, where soma (a mythical equivalent of semen)
is created by the gods in the form of foam produced by churning the ocean with an
uprooted mountain. Eros is to Aphrodite as desire is to its realization, and the con-
summation of male erotic desire is accompanied both by the emission of semen and
by an inevitable, if temporary, 'castration.' The names Kythereia and Kyprogenes,
as Hesiod says, are due to her associations with the islands Kythera and Cyprus,
which were early and famous centers of the worship of Aphrodite, whose most familiar title in Greek literature is Kypris [the Cyprian].

200 Philommeides [laughter-loving] is an early epithet of Aphrodite (*Iliad* 3.424, *Odyssey* 8.362, *Th* 989). Hesiod's pun, which derives this name from *medea* [geni-
tals], plays on the similarity in prononciation between the morphemes *meid*
[laughter] and *med* [genitals].

201 As an attendant of Aphrodite, Eros seems already to be changing from the cosmic
principle of 120 into his later role as companion and (usually) son of Aphrodite.
Himeros [Longing] is a double of Eros (see on 64).

when first she was born and went to join the gods.
She has such honor from the first, and this is her
province among men and immortal gods:
girls' whispers and smiles and deceptions,   205
sweet pleasure and sexual love and tenderness.
    Great Ouranos, their father, called his sons Titans,°
reproaching the sons whom he himself begot;
he said they strained in wickedness to do a
great wrong, but there would be revenge afterwards.   210
Nyx° bore hateful Moros° and black Ker and
Thanatos, she bore° Hypnos and the tribe of Oneiroi.
Next Momos and painful Oizys were born to
the dark goddess Nyx, though she lay with no one,
and the Hesperides who keep, beyond famous Okeanos,°   215

207-210 Hesiod derives the name *Titanes* from the verb *titaino* [strain]; there is also a
    secondary connection with *tisis* [revenge]. In the late rationalizing account of Dio-
    doros, who interpreted all myths as distorted versions of actual human history, the
    Titans got their name from their human mother Titaia, later called Gaia. Diodoros'
    strange version goes on to say the eldest daughters of Ouranos and Titaia were
    Basileia and Rhea (or Pandora). Basileia succeeded to the throne after her father's
    death and married her brother Hyperion, by whom she had two children, Helios and
    Selene. But her brothers, the Titans, murdered Hyperion and drowned Helios, at
    which Selene jumped to her death from a roof-top. Helios then appeared to Basileia
    in a vision and told her the Titans would be punished and that he and his sister
    would give their names to the sun and moon (formerly called "holy fire" and
    "mene"). Basileia then vanished from mortal sight and was honored as the Great
    Mother, and all the Titans were killed in a battle with Dionysos and his followers.
211-336 Before relating the families of the Titans, Hesiod returns to the first genera-
    tion and completes the story of the descendants of Nyx (211-232) and of Gaia and
    her son Pontos (233-336).
211 Moros [Doom], Ker [Destiny], and Thanatos [Death] each signify a different as-
    pect of death (West, *T* 227). All the children of Night are thematically associated
    with her in some way; they occur at night (e.g., Dreams, Love) or they are dark and
    terrible (e.g., Death, Pain, Discord) like "dark" (214) and "deadly" (223) Night her-
    self.
212-232 The remaining children of Night are personifications of Sleep [Hypnos],
    Dreams [Oneiroi], Blame [Momos], Pain [Oizys], Daughters of Night [Hesperides],
    Fates [Moirai], Destinies [Keres], Retribution [Nemesis], Deceit [Apate], Love
    [Philotes], Old Age [Geras], and Discord [Eris]. The children of Eris are Hardship
    [Ponos], Forgetfulness [Lethe], Starvation [Limos], Pains [Algea], Battles [Hysmi-
    nai], Wars [Machai], Murders [Phonoi], Manslaughters [Androktasiai], Quarrels
    [Neikea], Lies [Pseudea], Stories [Logoi], Disputes [Amphillogiai], Anarchy [Dys-
    nomia], Ruin [Ate], and Oath [Horkos].
215-216 The Hesperides are beautiful nymphs who, along with Atlas (517-520) and a
    monstrous serpent (334-335), guard the tree of golden apples in a marvelous gar-
    den somewhere in the imaginary world at the ends of the earth. A Hesiodic frag-

the beautiful gold apples and the fruit-bearing trees;
and she bore the Moirai and pitiless Keres,°
[Klotho and Lachesis and Atropos, who give to
mortals at birth both good and evil to have]
who pursue the sins of men and gods;   220
the goddesses never end their terrible anger
until they inflict evil on anyone who sins.
And deadly Nyx bore Nemesis,° a plague to mortal
men; after her she bore Apate and Philotes°
and painful Geras and hard-hearted Eris.°   225

---

ment says there were three Hesperides, named Aigle, Erytheia, and Hesperethousa,
but the third name is sometimes divided in half to make two nymphs, Hesperia and
Arethousa (*Ap* 2.5.11). The location of their garden is "beyond Okeanos" (215),
"toward Night" (275), "at the limits of the earth" (517); later, when the Greeks
knew more about the geography of remote places, they situated the garden somewhere beyond Mount Atlas in Morocco. The mythographer Pherekydes said that
Gaia gave the golden apple tree to Zeus and Hera as a wedding present, and Gaia
asked that it be planted in the garden. The garden of the Hesperides is a paradise
like Homer's "Elysian plain" or the situation of Hesiod's Golden Race (*WD* 109-
120). Although its descriptions are similar to those of the human paradises, it is a
garden of the gods and not of men; its ultimate souce may be the Sumerian garden
of the gods called Dilmun (*ANET* 37-41). The capture of the golden apples is the
objective of Herakles' eleventh labor, and they also appear in two myths connected
with marriage: Melanion (or Hippomenes) uses them to delay the pursuit of
Atalante and thus wins her hand in marriage (Ap 3.9.2), and the appearance of an
inscribed golden apple at the marriage of Thetis and Peleus begins the chain of
events which culminates in the Trojan War (Hyginus, *Fabula* 92).

217-219 Hesiod later calls the Moirai the daughters of Zeus and Themis (904), and
gives them the names which they traditionally have, but the names seem here to be
assigned to the Keres. They must, however, belong to the Moirai; 218-219 are almost identical to a later description of the Moirai (905-906) and may have been inserted here from the later passage by an editor or commentator who wanted to
balance the description of the Keres in 220-222 with a prior description of the Moirai. The Keres are a plural form of the singular Ker in 211, and both Keres and
Moirai represent the destined end of life.

223 Nemesis, the Erinyes, the Moirai, and the Keres are essentially personifications of
different aspects of human mortality. The special role of Nemesis is to punish ex-
cess, whether of good or of evil, and in this leveling function she is the agent of
Zeus, who "crushes the strong," "lowers the high," and "withers the proud" (*WD* 5-
7). Nemesis represents the fundamental Greek conception that anyone who rises
too high exposes himself to the envy and vengeance of the gods. The famous shrine
of Nemesis near Marathon in Attika contained a statue of the goddess which the
sculptor Phidias made from a block of Parian marble; the invading Persians had
brought the marble, intending to set up a trophy after they defeated the Athenians.

224 Deceit and Love appear together because, in Hesiod's view, they belong together.

225 Old Age personifies a stage of life portrayed often in Greek poetry, especially in
the poems attributed to Anakreon, as a fate words than death. Eris [Discord] is the
spirit of enmity and conflict who "advances evil war and battle" (*WD* 14), and who

And hateful Eris bore painful Ponos,
Lethe and Limos and the tearful Algea,
Hysminai, Machai, Phonoi, and Androktasiai;
Neikea, Pseudea, Logoi, and Amphillogiai,
Dysnomia and Ate, near one another,°   230
and Horkos,° who most afflicts men on earth,
Then anyone willingly swears a false oath.
Pontos begot Nereus,° truthful and never false,
eldest of his children; he is called the Old Man
since he is true and gentle; what is lawful   235
he remembers, and he knows just and gentle thoughts.°
Then he begot great Thaumas° and proud Phorkys,
from union with Gaia, and fair-cheeked Keto, and
Eurybia, who has in her breast a heart of adamant.
    To Nereus were born numerous divine children   240
in the barren sea; their mother was fair-haired Doris,°
daughter of Okeanos, the full-circling river:

---

used a golden apple to start a conflict between three goddesses which led to the
Trojan War. In the *Works and Days* Hesiod reconsiders and says that she has an
older sister, also named Eris, who personifies healthy competition (11-26).

230 Ate is Doom resulting from delusion or misguided thinking. Homer, who calls her
the daughter of Zeus, tells how she deceived her father and was banished from
Olympos (*Iliad* 19. 85-138).

231 Oath is a negative concept because he represents the punishment one promises to
undergo if an oath is false (e.g., "if I am lying [or do not do what I say], may I be
punished").

233-236 Nereus is often called the "Old Man of the Sea" or simply the "Old Man,"
and he may be the extant mythical figure most closely related to a primordial oce-
anic father-god (see on 20). He is similar to, and may be the same as, other sea-dei-
ties called Proteus, Glaukos, and Phorkys. Since water-deities in general have the
ability to change their appearance and shape (water itself having no fixed shape),
this confusion is not surprising. The metamorphic power of these sea-gods is often
connected with their prophetic ability: Proteus turns into a lion, serpent, leopard,
boar, water, and a tree in his effort to avoid Menelaos' questions about the future
(*Odyssey* 4. 456-458); according to Pherekydes, Nereus changes into water and fire
before telling Herakles the directions to the garden of the Hesperides.

233-336 This long section lists the children who result from the union between Gaia
and Pontos, and their descendants.

237-238 Thaumas, Phorkys, and Keto will be the parents of monstrous and marvelous
offspring, and their names hint at this. *Thauma* means "marvel," *ketos* means
"whale" or "sea-monster," and *phoke* means "seal" (although *phorkys* and *phoke*
cannot be derived from one another linguistically, there is a certain sound-similar-
ity, and Proteus sleeps with a herd of seals in *Odyssey* 4).

241 The birth of Doris, mother of the Nereids, will be reported at 350.

Protho,° Eukrante, Sao, Amphitrite,°
Eudora, Thetis,° Galene, and Glauke,
Kymothoe, swift Speio, lovely Thalia,   245
Pasithea, Erato, and rose-armed Eunike,
graceful Melite, Eulimene, Agaue,
Doto, Proto, Pherousa, and Dynamene,
Nesaia, Aktaia, and Protomedeia,
Doris and Panope and shapely Galateia,°   250
lovely Hippothoe, rose-armed Hipponoe,
Kymodoke, who easily calms waves on the windy
sea and the blowing of windy gales,
with Kymatolege and fine-ankled Amphitrite,°
and Kymo, Eione, and well-crowned Halimede,   255
Glaukonome, who loves smiles, and Pontoporeia,
Leiagora and Euagora and Laomedeia,
Poulynoe and Autonoe and Lysianassa,
Euarne of lovely shape and blameless form,
Psamathe° of graceful body, divine Menippe,   260
Neso, Eupompe, Themisto, and Pronoe, and
Nemertes, who has the mind of her immortal father.
These were the daughters of blameless Nereus:
fifty girls, skilled in blameless works.
　　Thaumas° married deep-flowing Okeanos'   265

243-264 The fifty Nereid nymphs are representations of the beautiful and positive aspects of the sea and appear in myth usually as attractive spectators. Nereids of individual significance are Amphitrite (243), Thetis (244), Galateia (250), and Psamathe (260).

243 Amphitrite will be the wife of Poseidon at 930.

244 Thetis is the most famous Nereid. When Zeus learnsshe is fated to bear a son who will be greater than his father, he forces her to marry the mortal Peleus. The son of Thetis and Peleus is Achilleus, and Thetis plays a major role in the *Iliad* as protector and advisor of her son. Thetis personifies the good and nurturant mother; she also saves and raises Hephaistos when Hera throws him out of Olympos (*Iliad* 18. 395-398), and similarly gives refuge in the sea to Dionysos (*Ap* 3.6.1). Estranged from her husband Peleus after the birth of Achilleus, she nevertheless appears to him on several occasions, most notably when he is one of the Argonauts and she and the other Nereids guide the ship Argo through the Clashing Rocks (*Ap* 1.9.25).

250 Galateia is the object of the Kyklops Polyphemos' unrequited love in *Theokritos* 11.

254 Why Amphitrite appears both here and at 243 is a mystery.

260 Psamathe will marry Aiakos and bear a son Phokos (1003-1005). Psamathe changes into a seal in her effort to resist the advances of Aiakos *Ap* 3.12.6); hence the name of her son Phokos (from phoke, "seal.")

265 Like his brother Nereus, Thaumas marries a daughter of Okeanos.

daughter Elektra;° she bore swift Iris
and the fair-haired Harpies,° Aello and Okypete,
who fly as the birds and gusts of winds
on swift wings, rushing high in the air.

    Keto bore to Phorkys the fair-cheeked hags,   270
grey from birth, who are called the Graiai°
by immortal gods and men who go on earth,
fine-robed Pemphredo and saffron-robed Enyo,
and the Gorgons,° who live beyond famous Okeanos,
at the limit toward Night, with the clear-voiced   275
Hesperides, Sthenno, Euryale, and unlucky Medousa;

---

266 The birth of Elektra appears in 349. Iris is the personification of the rainbow and, since the rainbow seems to connect sky and earth, she is a messenger between gods and men.

267-269 The Harpies are storm-wind spirits. They appear on grave stones carrying the souls of the dead, and are said to have carried off the daughters of Pandareos (*Odyssey* 20.77). To be "carried away by the stormwinds [*thyellai*]" or "by the Harpies" seems to mean "to disappear" or "to die." They appear in art with the body of a bird and the breast and face of a woman (like the Seirenes). In the Argonaut myth, they are the persecutors of the blind prophet Phineus (*Ap* 1.9.21). The name *harpyia* is related to the verb *harpazo* [snatch, carry off] and perhaps also to *harpe* [sickle, bird of prey]; the mythographer Parthenios calls Eros "Harpys," and a fragment of the lyric poet Alkman calls Eros the son of Iris and nephew of the Harpies.

270-273 The two Graiai, Pemphredo and Enyo, have in later accounts a third sister, usually named Deino (*Ap* 2.4.2). According to Apollodoros, they have only one eye and one tooth between them, which they pass to whichever one wants to see or eat; Perseus steals the eye and tooth and compels the Graiai to help him in his search for Medousa. The Graiai are grey-haired at birth, as are the babies born at the end of the Iron Race (*WD* 181). That they are both grey-haired and "fair-cheeked" is typical of the ambivalence which often characterizes female monsters in Greek myth; the Graiai, the Gorgon Medousa, the viper-woman Echidna, and even the Erinyes can be both beautiful and hideous.

274-276 The Gorgons, like the Graiai, are known for their part in the myth of Perseus, who is sent by the king Polydektes to bring back the head of Medousa. They live in that imaginary land far to the west (beyond the ocean) where other fantastic and monstrous creatures dwell; Hesiod places them near (or in) the garden of the Hesperides. Apollodoros (2.4.2) describes them as having snakes for hair, tusks like a boar, bronze hands, and golden wings. If a Gorgon looks at someone looking at her (i.e., if their eyes meet), that person is turned to stone. Underlying this punishment must be a fantasy of the danger involved if one is caught looking at a forbidden sight; such a fantasy typically originates in childhood and the forbidden sight is presumably sexual in nature. Parallel mythical incidents are the punishments of Teiresias and Aktaion, who are blinded and torn to pieces, respectively, for accidentally seeing a goddess naked (*Ap* 3.6.7, 3.4.4). According to Pausanias (8.47), even a lock of Medousa's hair could rout an entire army.

she was mortal, but they were immortal and ageless,°
both of them; the Dark-Haired god° lay with her
in a soft meadow and flowers of spring.
And when Perseus cut off her head, out   280
jumped great Chrysaor° and the horse Pegasos,
who has this name° since by the springs of Okeanos
he was born, and the other holds a gold sword in his hands;
he° flew off and left the earth, mother of flocks,
and came to the immortals; he lives in the house   285
of wise Zeus and carries his thunder and lightning.
Chrysaor begot three-headed Geryoneus,° from union
with Kallirhoe, daughter of famous Okeanos.
Mighty Herakles killed Geryoneus° by his
rolling-gaited cattle in sea-washed Erytheia   290
on the very day he drove the wide-faced cattle
to holy Tiryns, having crossed the ford of Okeanos
and killed Orthos and the herdsman Eurytion
in the misty stable beyond famous Okeanos.

---

277 The discrepancy between Medousa's mortality and her sisters' immortality is
compared by West (*T*, 246) to the status of Kastor and Polyneikes, but these two
brothers had different fathers; a more appropriate parallel is the monstrous Ler-
naian Hydra (314-315), who had eight mortal heads and one immortal head (*Ap*
2.5.2).

278-279 The "Dark-Haired" god is Poseidon, and the "soft meadow and flowers of
spring" indicate that the site of this union, and perhaps the permanent home of the
Gorgons, is the garden of the Hesperides. In the attraction Medousa holds for
Poseidon, we see again the beauty/ugliness ambivalence of some female monsters,
their capacity to inspire both desire and fear. The destructive power of the Gorgons
is also subject to ambivalence: blood drawn from their left-hand veins brings instant death, while blood from the right-hand veins can restore the dead to life (*Ap*
3.10.3).

280-281 Chrysaor and Pegasos, the children of Medousa and Poseidon, seem to be
born from her head rather than from her trunk.

282-283 Pegasos is named for springs [*pegai*] and Chrysaor for the weapon he carries
at his birth, a golden sword [*chryseon aor*].

284-286 Pegasos is best known as the winged horse on which Bellerophon rides to his
heroic victories (Pindar, *Olympian* 13), but his usual home is the stables of Zeus.

287-288 The birth of Kallirhoe is at 351. Geryoneus, who appears on vase paintings as
three warriors joined together side by side, is usually called "triple-bodied" (as in
Aeschylus, Agamemnon 870) rather than "three-headed."

289-294 Geryoneus also lives in the imaginary far west; his island Erytheia (also the
name of one of the Hesperides) is somewhere in the Atlantic. The tenth labor of
Herakles is to capture the cattle of Geryoneus and bring them to Eurystheus at
Tiryns. To ferry the cattle from island to mainland, Herakles uses the golden cup of

She° bore another unbeatable monster, in no way   295
like mortal men or immortal gods, in a
hollow cave, the divine and hard-hearted Echidna,
half a nymph with glancing eyes and lovely cheeks,
half a monstrous snake, terrible and great, a
shimmering flesh-eater in the dark holes of holy earth.   300
There she has a cave, down under the hollow rock,
far from the immortal gods and mortal men; there
the gods allotted to her a famous house to live in.
    Grim Echidna watches in Arima under the earth,°
an immortal and ageless nymph for all days.°   305
They say that Typhoeus° was joined in love with her,
the arrogant and lawless monster with the glancing girl;
she conceived and bore strong-hearted children:
first she bore Orthos, the dog of Geryoneus;°
next she bore the unfightable and unspeakable   310
flesh-eating Kerberos,° bronze-voiced dog of Hades,
fifty-headed, pitiless and strong;
third she bore the ill-intended Hydra° of

---

    the Sun; to win the cattle he has to kill Geryoneus, his monstrous dog Orthos (309), and his herdsman Eurytion.

295-303 "She" is presumably Keto. Echidna is another ambivalently-regarded hybrid, half-serpent and half-nymph. Hesiod does not specify which half is which, but the viper-maiden met by Herakles is described by Herodotos (4.8-10) as a woman from the buttocks up and a serpent below. This would conform with other composite monsters (Harpies, Sphinx, etc.); if they are part-woman, the upper part is human (since this is the part of the mother with which the male child is familiar; the other, lower part is unseen, therefore exciting curiosity and fantasy).

304 The location of Arima (or perhaps "the Arimoi") is unknown, although it is associated with Typhoeus, Echidna's husband, by Homer (*Iliad* 2.783).

305 Although Hesiod calls Echidna immortal, her death is told by Apollodoros (2.1.2).

306-308 Typhoeus is the greatest monster of them all, and Zeus' most formidable enemy (820-868). The union of Echidna and Typhoeus will produce four offspring who take after their hundred-headed father (825) in their own variable multiplicity of heads.

309 Orthos is a two-headed dog (*Ap* 2.5.10).

310-312 Kerberos guards the entrance to the underworld, refusing to let inmates out or visitors in. Various sources give him from three to a hundred heads. Herakles' twelfth and final labor is to bring Kerberos up from Hades.

313-318 The number of the Hydra's heads ranges from one to a hundred, with nine as the usual number; her appearance is like that of an octopus, with a head at the end of each tentacle. The second labor of Herakles is to kill the Hydra, but he found that two new heads grew whenever he knocked one off. Since the Hydra was aided by a giant crab, Herakles also received assistance from his nephew Iolaos, who

Lerna, whom the white-armed goddess Hera raised
in her infinite anger against mighty Herakles;   315
she died by the unfeeling bronze sword of Herakles,
son of Zeus and stepson of Amphitryon, with war-loving
Iolaos, by the plans of army-leading Athena.
She° bore Chimaira, who breathes furious fire,
terrible and great, swift-footed and strong,   320
with three headsone of a hard-eyed lion,
one of a goat, one of a snake, a strong serpent;
[a lion in front, a snake behind, a goat in between,
breathing the terrible strength of blazing fire]
Pegasos and noble Bellerophon killed her.   325
And she° bore the deadly Sphinx, destroyer of the Kadmeians,
from union with Orthos, and the Nemeian lion°
whom Hera, noble wife of Zeus, raised and
settled in the hills of Nemeia, a plague to men.
There he lived and ravaged the tribes of men,   330
master of Nemeian Tretos and Apesas, but
the great strength of Herakles overcame him.
　　Keto joined in love with Phorkys and bore her youngest,°

---

cauterized the necks with a torch and prevented new heads from sprouting. Hera's
hostility is a recurrent feature of the myth of Herakles, her most hated stepson; she
also deprives him of his birthright, sends serpents to strangle him in his crib, incites
the Amazons against him, and drives him mad.

319-325 The ambiguous "she" is probably Echidna, not Hydra. The word chimaira
means "he-goat." Lines 323-324 are bracketed because they repeat exactly *Iliad*
6.181-182; they suggest that Homer, at least, believed the lion's head grew from
the monster's neck, the goat's from its back, and the serpent's was its tail. Killing
Chimaira was the trial imposed on Bellerophon by the Lykian king Iobates (*Iliad*
6.155-183). According to the Byzantine critic Tzetzes (on *Lykophron* 17), Bellerophon used his spear to lodge a piece of lead in Chimaira's throat; when her fiery
breath melted the lead, she swallowed it and died.

326 "She" could be either Echidna or Chimaira. The Sphinx (or Phix, in Hesiod's
Boiotian dialect) has the body of a lion, wings, and the head and breast of a
woman. The Kadmeians are the Thebans (named after Kadmos, founder of Thebes), and the Sphinx is called their destroyer because she killed and ate whoever
could not answer her famous riddle. When Oidipous finally answered correctly, she
leapt from a height to her death (a strange sort of suicide for a winged creature).

327-332 The brother of the Sphinx is the Nemeian lion, raised by Hera (like the Hydra) as a weapon in her animosity against Herakles. Herakles' first labor was to kill
this lion, a task made more difficult by the fact that the lion's skin could not be
pierced. Herakles therefore strangled it and from then on wore the lion-skin as his
familiar cloak. Tretos and Apesas are mountains between Mycenae and Corinth.

a terrible serpent in the recesses of dark earth,
at the great limits, who guards the all-golden apples.   335
And this is the progeny from Keto and Phorkys.°
     Tethys bore to Okeanos the swirling Rivers,°
Neilos, Alpheios, and deep-whirling Eridanos,
Strymon, Maiandros, and fair-flowing Istros,
Phasis, Rhesos, and silver-swirling Acheloos,   340
Nessos, Rhodios, Haliakmon, Heptaporos,
Granikos, Aisepos, and divine Simois,
Peneios, Hermos, and fair-flowing Kaikos,
great Sangarios, Ladon, and Parthenios,
Euenos, Aldeskos, and divine Skamandros.   345
And she bore a holy race of Kourai,° who on earth
raise youths to manhood, with lord Apollo
and the Rivers, holding this duty from Zeus:
Peitho, Admete, Ianthe, and Elektra,°
Doris, Prymno, and Ourania of divine form,°   350
Hippo, Klymene, Rhodeia, and Kallirhoe,°
Zeuxo, Klytia, Idyia, and Pasithoe,
Plexaura, Galaxaura, and beautiful Dione,°

332-335 The final child of Keto and Phorkys is the huge serpent who guards the apples
of the Hesperides. Apollonios (*Argonautika* 4.1396) calls him Ladon and says he is
a son of Gaia; Apollodoros (2.5.11) says he has a hundred heads and speaks with
many voices (like Typhoeus, *Th* 829-835). One of the rivers born from Okeanos
will be named Ladon (344).

336 Hesiod now comes to the families of the Titans, beginning with the children of
Okeanos and Tethys. The sons are rivers and the daughters are nymphs of springs.

337-345 Neilos is the Nile, and Eridanos and Phasis are legendary rivers. As for the
other 22 named rivers, they are identified by West (*T*, 259) as "divided between
Greece (Acheloos, Alpheios, Peneios, Ladon, Haliakmon, Euenos), Greek Asia Minor (Maiandros, Hermos, Kaikos), the Troad (Skamandros, Simois, Aisepos,
Rhesos, Heptaporos, Rhodios, Granikos), Aegean Thrace (Strymon, Nessos), and
the south and west shores of the Black Sea (Istros, Aldeskos, Sangarios,
Parthenios)."

346-348 The Okeanid nymphs, daughters of Okeanos and Tethys, are not called
Okeanides, but later *Okeaninai* (364) and here simply kourai [daughters, girls,
maidens], a title which suggests their function of raising youths [*kourizousi*, 347].
This function must be connected with cult practices which put child-rearing under
the sponsorship of legendary guardians of local springs and rivers, along with
Apollo.

349 Peitho is the personification of Persuasion; in *WD* 73, she helps to dress and deco-
rate Pandora. Elektra is the wife of Thaumas (265-266).

350 Doris is the mother of the Nereid nymphs (241). Ourania is also the name of a
Muse (78).

Melobosis, Thoe, and fair-figured Polydora,
Kerkeis, beautiful of form, and cow-eyed Plouto,   355
Perseis, Ianeira, Akaste, and Xanthe,
lovely Petraia, Menestho, Europe,
Metis, Eurynome, and saffron-robed Telesto,°
Chryseis, Asia, and desirable Kalypso,°
Eudora, Tyche,° Amphirho, and Okyrhoe,   360
and Styx,° who is most eminent of all.
These were born from Okeanos and Tethys,°
the eldest daughters; but there are also many others,
for Okeanos has three thousand slender-ankled daughters
who, scattered over the earth and watery depths,   365
serve everywhere alike, glorious divine children.
There are as many other rivers, noisily-flowing
sons of Okeanos, whom mistress Tethys bore;
it is hard for a man to say the names of them all,
but individuals know the ones by which they live.   370
Theia bore° great Helios and bright Selene
and Eos, who shines upon all the earth and
upon the immortal gods who hold the wide sky,
after Theia was won in love by Hyperion.
　　Divine Eurybia° joined in love with Kreios and   375
bore Astraios and great Pallas and Perses,°

---

351 Hippo must be one of the springs created by the kick of Pegasos [*hippos* = horse].
　　Klymene will be the wife of the Titan Iapetos (506-507).

353 For Dione see on 17.

358 Metis [wisdom, counsel] will be Zeus' first wife (886), and Eurynome will be his
　　third (907). Eurynome and Thetis save Hephaistos when he is thrown from the sky
　　by Hera (*Iliad* 18.395-398); see *Ps* 99.

359 Asia is the wife of the Titan Iapetos in *Ap* 1.2.3, and of Prometheus in Herodotos
　　4.45 (and in Shelley's *Prometheus Unbound*). Kalypso is probably not the famous
　　Kalypso of *Odyssey* 5, who is usually called the daughter of Atlas (*Odyssey* 1.52).

360 Tyche is the personification of Chance.

361 Styx, who is named last, is the eldest Okeanid (776). Why Styx is "most eminent"
　　is explained in 389-401 and 782-806.

362-370 The 6000 children of Okeanos and Tethys easily make them the most prolific
　　of Greek divinities, another hint of their possible role as a primal couple.

371-374 The children of the Titans Theia and Hyperion are Helios [Sun], Selene
　　[Moon], and Eos [Dawn].

375 Eurybia is the hard-hearted daughter of Gaia and Pontos (239).

376 Astraios is an appropriate name for the father of the Stars (382); Pallas will be the
　　husband of Styx (383); Perses will be the father of Hekate (409-411).

who stands out among all for his knowledge.°
To Astraios Eos bore the strong-hearted winds,
cleansing Zephyros and swift-running Boreas,°
and Notos,° a goddess united in love with a god;   380
after these Erigeneia bore the star Eosphoros°
and the shining Stars the sky wears as a crown.
Styx, daughter of Okeanos, lay with Pallas and bore°
Zelos and fine-ankled Nike in the house;
and she bore famous children, Kratos and Bia,   385
whose house is not apart from Zeus; they neither sit
nor go, except where the god should lead them,
but always are stationed by deep-thundering Zeus.
This is what immortal Styx, daughter of Okeanos, planned°
on that day when the Olympian lightning-holder   390
called all the immortal gods to vast Olympos
and said whichever gods with him would fight the Titans
would not lose their rights, but each would have
the honor he held before among the immortal gods.
He said that whoever held no honor or right under Kronos   395
would enter upon honor and rights, as is just.
First immortal Styx came to Olympos°
with her children, by the advice of her father;°
Zeus honored her and gave outstanding gifts.°
He set her to be the gods' great oath and°   400
gave to her children to live with him for all days.
Just as he promised, to all without fail he

---

377 The outstanding knowledge of Perses contrasts with the outstanding foolishness of
  another Perses, Hesiod's brother (*WD* 286, 397, 633).
379 Zephyros is the west wind, Boreas the north wind.
380 Notos is the south wind.
381 Erigeneia [Early-Born] is a title of Eos [Dawn]. Eosphoros [Dawn-Bringer] is Ve-
  nus, the Morning Star.
383-387 The children of Styx and Pallas are the personifications Zelos [Envy], Nike
  [Victory], Kratos [Power], and Bia [Force], who continually attend Zeus.
389-396 The politic Zeus promises to any god who will help him in the war against the
  Titans that he will not take away offices from previous office-holders and that he
  will give offices to any who do not have them.
397 Olympos is the headquartes of Zeus' faction in the Titanomachy (633).
398 Okeanos' treason against his brother Titans suggests again that in some version he
  is not really a Titan (see on 20).
399 Zeus treats Styx in the same way that he will treat Hekate (412).
400 See 782-806.

fulfilled; as for himself, he rules with great power.

Phoibe° came to Koios' bed of much desire;
the goddess, pregnant by the god's love,   405
bore dark-robed Leto,° always sweet
and gentle to men and immortal gods,
sweet from the first, most mild in Olympos.
She also bore remarkable Asteria,° whom Perses
led to his great house to be called his wife.   410
She conceived and bore Hekate,° whom above all
Zeus, Kronos' son, honored; he gave her notable gifts,°
to have a share of the earth and barren sea.
She also has a share of honor from the starry sky,
and is honored most of all by the immortal gods.   415
For even now, whenever someone of men on earth
sacrifices fine things and prays in due ritual,
he invokes Hekate; much honor comes to him
very easily, whose prayers the goddess favorably
receives, and she grants him wealth, since this is   420
her power. For as many were born of Gaia and Ouranos°

---

404 Phoibe's name seems connected with (perhaps derived from) that of her grandson
Phoibos Apollo.

406 Leto will be Zeus' sixth wife, and the mother of Apollo and Artemis (918-920).

409 Phoibe's other daughter Asteria has the same name as the island (later called Delos) where Leto gives birth to Apollo and Artemis (*Ap* 1.4.1). Since Delos was also
known as Ortygia, Apollodoros has Asteria change herself into a quail [ortyx] to
avoid the advances of Zeus. Stories like this support the version attributed to
Mousaios that Perses was the husband of Asteria, but Zeus was the father of
Hekate.

411-452 The great emphasis put on the worship of Hekate and on her omnipresent
power is best explained (with West, *T* 276-280) as due to Hesiod's personal interest
in the goddess. The Hekate cult seems to have come to Greece from Karia in Asia
Minor; if Hesiod's father was a member of the cult, this may explain why he named
his other son Perses, the same name as Hekate's father. Despite the extensive praise
given to Hekate, we should not suppose that Hesiod regarded her as equal to, or
above, the major Olympian deities. Her status was presumably more like that of a
patron saint, to whom one prays for special favors as well as for regular guidance
and success in various ventures.

412 There seems to be an intentional parallel between Hekate and Styx, who also received honor and "outstanding gifts" from Zeus (399). Styx seems to have the same
function among the gods as Hekate does among mortals; each of them is invoked
on particular occasions, Styx for the oath of the gods (400) and Hekate for concrete
favors (416-421, 429-447).

421-425 Again Hekate is similar to Styx, in that each maintains the rights and powers
she held before the reign of Zeus (Styx in 392-394).

and obtained honor, among them all she has her due;
Kronos' son neither wronged her nor took away
what she received among the Titans, the former gods,
but this she keeps, as was the division at the beginning.   425
Nor, since she is an only child,° does the goddess obtain
less honor and privileges on earth and sky and sea,
but rather she has still more, for Zeus honors her.
Greatly she assists and benefits whom she will;°
she sits by reverent kings in judgment, and he is   430
eminent among the people in assembly, whom she wishes;
whenever men arm for man-killing war, then
the goddess is there, and to whom she wishes
she gladly grants victory and extends glory.
She is good to stand by cavalry, by whom she wishes;   435
she is also good when men compete in the contest;°
then also the goddess assists and benefits them;
one who wins by might and strength bears off the fine
prize easily and happily, and brings glory to his parents.
To those who work the grey sea's discomfort°   440
and pray to Hekate and loud-sounding Earth-Shaker,
the noble goddess easily grants much catch, and
easily takes it back when it appears, if her heart wishes.
She is good, with Hermes, to increase the stock in barns;
herds of cattle and wide herds of goats and   445
flocks of wooly sheep, if her spirit wishes,
she increases from few and from many makes less.
So even though being her mother's only child, she
is honored with privileges among all the immortals.
Kronos' son made her guardian of the young, who after   450
her saw with their eyes the light of much-seeing Eos.
So always she guards the young, and these are her honors.°

---

426 Concern for the status of Hekate as an only child seems to be an extension to the
divine realm of the precarious civic and legal status of a single female child in human society.

429-435 These lines may well be intended for Hesiod's audience, the rulers of Chalkis.

436-439 These lines also point to the occasion of the Chalkis contest, and express Hesiod's hope that the goddess will grant him victory.

440-447 That Hekate can either increase or decrease a fisherman's catch, or the
number of a farmer's animals, suggests that her role is not only to help when invoked; she also can harm those who ignore her.

450-452 Hekate's role as guardian of the young associates her with Apollo, her cousin,
and also with the Okeanid nymphs, including Styx (see on 364-368).

Rhea lay with Kronos and bore illustrious children:°
Hestia,° Demeter, and gold-sandaled Hera and
strong Hades,° who lives in a palace under the ground   455
and has a pitiless heart, and loud-sounding Earth-Shaker°

453-506 Coming now to Kronos and Rhea, Hesiod rejoins the story of the succession myth. We would expect the family of Kronos to come last, since Kronos is the youngest of the Titans, but Hesiod puts Kronos before Iapetos so that Zeus' victory can be mentioned before telling the story of Iapetos' son Prometheus (a story in which Zeus is already king of the gods). This part of the succession myth is based largely on two identifiable sources, the Near Eastern myths of divine conflict and Minoan myths of the birth of a god in a mountain cave. For the logic of Hesiod's version, see *In* 16-17; for its psychological meaning see *Ps* 95-97.

454 Hestia, the eldest daughter of Kronos and Rhea, has virtually no mythical function or role. The *Hh to Aphrodite* mentions her, along with the other two famous virgin goddesses Athena and Artemis, as untouched by the "works of Aphrodite." Courted by both Poseidon and Apollo, she swore to Zeus that she would remain a virgin always; instead of marriage Zeus gave to her the right of being the goddess of the hearth. The hearth was the center of ritual; the city hearth, site of civic ritual, represented for the entire population what the private hearth in each home meant to the individual and family. Its fire was not allowed to go out and every day it was the focus (Latin *focus* = hearth) of ritual activities such as food offerings and libations. Like Hesiod's Hekate, Hestia is connected with actual everyday life, and like Hekate she is said to have received high honor among gods and mortals (*Hh to Aphrodite* 29-32). Demeter, the second daughter, is primarily a goddess of grain, vegetation, and fertility. She is best known in the myth of the loss and recovery of her daughter Persephone, carried off by Hades to be his bride in the underworld but ultimately restored to her mother. While Demeter mourns the loss of Persephone, nothing grows; upon their reunion the earth bursts into bloom. Demeter is a maternal goddess, but in a special sense: she is the mother lost by the child and the mother to whom one hopes to return. She will be Zeus' fourth wife (912-914). Hera, Zeus' seventh and final wife (921), is primarily a goddess of weddings and marriage in Greek cult. In myth she is the powerful wife of Zeus, but both her power and her status as wife are more negative than positive. She is rarely maternal (see on 922), but is usually a hostile and resentful stepmother. Her anger is aimed chiefly at Zeus' many illegitimate children, whose rise to heroic status is in large part the result of their attempts to resist, avoid, or placate her fury. As a wife she is usually portrayed as jealous and spiteful, and on two occasions she bears parthenogenic sons (Hephaistos and Typhoeus) as a direct result of her desire for revenge against her husband; see *Ps* 99-101.

455 Hades is the god of death and the underworld; his name seems to mean the "Unseen One" and the Greeks were generally reluctant to call him by name, preferring instead to use euphemisms like "Master of Many," "Receiver of Many," and the "Rich One" [Polysemantor, Polydegmon, Plouton]. He appears rarely in myth, since he rarely leaves his underworld palace; the one notable exception is his brief appearance on earth to carry off Demeter's daughter Persephone.

456 Poseidon, the "Earth-Shaker," is the chief among several gods of the sea; we have already seen Pontos, Okeanos, and Nereus, and there are others. Poseidon is also associated with earthquakes and with horses; he is frequently called Poseidon Hip-

and wise Zeus,° the father of gods and men,
by whose thunder the wide earth is shaken.
Great Kronos° would swallow these, as each
would come from the holy womb to his mother's knees,°   460
intending this, that none of Ouranos' proud line° but
himself would hold the right of king over the immortals.
For he learned from Gaia and starry Ouranos°
that it was fate that his own son would overthrow him,
although he was powerful, by the plans of great Zeus.   465
So he kept no blind man's watch, but alertly
swallowed his own children; incurable grief held Rhea.

[handwritten margin note: After gaining power, Zeus gains sexual access - 465]

---

pios [Horse Poseidon]. Perhaps his connection with the sea is a secondary development, which occurred after the Greeks entered the Mediterranean region and encountered the sea; such an important domain (both geographically and economically) must be made the domain of one of Zeus' brothers. In general Poseidon, like the storm-god Zeus, is a god of force; he is the god who brings sea-storms and earthquakes (or averts their harm), and in his sexual encounters he overcomes monsters such as Medousa or takes the form of a stallion. His emblem is the phallic trident, a counterpart to Zeus' lightning.

457-458 Zeus is a sky-god like his grandfather Ouranos, associated especially with rain, storms, and lightning. He is king of the gods because he is most powerful, but he is also most wise. He seems to be connected with no particular city or region, but is the most panhellenic of the gods. He is also the most sexually active; Okeanos may have more children, but almost all are from the same wife, whereas Zeus fathers many children by many wives and in many different metamorphoses. As in the myth of Semele (*Ps* 94), his sexuality, his strength, and his rule converge in the symbol of his irresistible lightning.

459-467 For Kronos' strategy see *In* 15-17 and *Ps* 95-96. There are similarities between the story of Kronos swallowing his children and the Hurrian myth of Kumarbi and the children who grew inside him; there are also important differences (*In* 24-26).

460 The Greek word for "knee" [*gonu*] is related to various words referring to the organs and process of generation: *gone* is "semen" (*WD* 733), *gonos* is "child" (*Th* 919), *goneus* is "begetter" (*WD* 235), etc. In *Hh to Apollo*, Leto gives birth to Apollo from a kneeling position (117).

461-462 Kronos' motive for confining his children is explicitly stated, since it requires an independent action (swallowing them); Ouranos, on the other hand, kept his children pent up in their mother's body by his incessant intercourse. For both of them, sexual dominance seems to be the underlying purpose in their treatment of their children.

463-465 Gaia and Ouranos foretell, but do not determine, the future. Their prophecy to Kronos may put him on the alert, but his efforts will necessarily fail. Gaia's prophetic power appears again in the statement by Aeschylus (*Eumenides* 1-8) that she was the first god of the Delphic oracle, followed by Themis, Phoibe, and finally Apollo. Ouranos is not usually credited with prophetic powers, but in the myth of Kumarbi it is Anu, the Hurrian counterpart of Ouranos, who predicts to Kumarbi his downfall (*In* 21).

But when she was about to bear Zeus, father of gods°
and men, she begged her own dear parents,
Gaia and starry Ouranos, to help her think   470
of a plan, by which she might secretly have
her son, and make great crafty Kronos pay the
Erinyes of her father and the children he swallowed.
They heard and obeyed their dear daughter
and told her what was destined to happen   475
concerning king Kronos and his strong-hearted son.
They sent her to Lyktos, to the rich land of Crete,°
when she was about to bear her youngest son,
great Zeus; vast Gaia received him from her
in wide Crete to tend and raise.   480
Carrying him through the swift black night, she came°
first to Lyktos; taking him in her arms, she hid him
in a deep cave, down in dark holes of holy earth,
on Mount Aigaion, dense with woods.

468-476 Gaia and Ouranos prophesy also to Rhea; their revelation is the same one they gave to Kronos. More importantly, Gaia actively assists her and thus plays a role in the fulfillment of her prophecy. The Erinyes are the spirits of guilt and retribution whose presence is the result of Kronos' misdeeds against his father and his children (see on 178-187).

477 At this point the Greek version of the Near Eastern succession myth begins to merge with a Minoan myth of a divine child. The myth of Zeus' birth in Crete is clearly derived from the Aegean cults which preceded the arrival in Greece of Indo-Europeans and their sky-god. In the Bronze Age matriarchal religion of Crete, there seems to have been a cult in honor of a male fertility-spirit, who was born and died each year. He may have been represented sometimes as the bull who appears so prominently in Minoan iconography, sometimes as a young man later named Kouros, the consort (and perhaps son) of the mother goddess. As various parts of the Aegean religion were assimilated into the beliefs of the Greeks, the cult of Kouros was replaced by that of Zeus. A thousand years after the end of Minoan civilization, Zeus is still addressed as the "greatest Kouros" in a hymn from Palaikastro in east Crete, and there was even a tomb on Crete in which Zeus was supposedly buried. Lyktos is a town near Mount Lasithi in east-central Crete.

481-484 Mount Aigaion (the "Aegean Mountain") is probably an ancient name for Mount Lasithi [if the Greek text is correct]). The cave in which Zeus was hidden by Gaia may be Psychro, a cave high on the Lasithi Plateau (still advertised to tourists today as the birthplace of Zeus). For details about the various Lasithi caves, see West, *T* 297-298. Ancient writers other than Hesiod located the Cretan cave of Zeus on Mount Ida to the west or Mount Dikte to the east, neither of them near Lyktos; Apollodoros (1.1.6) resolves the problem by naming the mountain Dikte and one of Zeus' nurses Ida.

Rhea° wrapped a huge stone in a baby's robe, and fed it   485
to Ouranos' wide-ruling son, king of the earlier gods;
he took it in his hands and put it down his belly,
the fool; he did not think in his mind that instead
of a stone his own son, undefeated and secure, was left
behind, soon to overthrow him by force and violence and   490
drive him from his honor, and rule the immortals himself.
    Swiftly then° the strength and noble limbs
of the future lord grew; at the end of a year,
tricked by the clever advice of Gaia,°
great crafty Kronos threw up his children,   495
defeated by the craft and force of his own son.
First he vomited out the stone° he had swallowed last;
Zeus fixed it firmly in the wide-pathed earth
at sacred Pytho in the vales of Parnassos,
to be a sign thereafter, a wonder to mortal men.   500
    He released from their deadly chains his uncles,°
Ouranos' sons, whom their father mindlessly bound.
They did not forget gratitude for his help,

485-488 The trick of Rhea may have a parallel in the myth of Kumarbi, who, with
    three gods already inside him, asks for a "son" (or a "stone") to eat; unfortunately
    the text here (column ii 39-54, *ANET* 121) is so badly preserved that it can scarcely
    be read at all. According to Pausanias, a local Arcadian legend said that Rhea had
    earlier hidden Poseidon among lambs and given Kronos a foal to swallow instead
    of Poseidon (8.8), and several places (e.g., Mount Thaumasios in Arcadia, 8.36;
    Mount Petrachos in Boiotia, 9.41) were claimed by local inhabitants to be the place
    where Rhea gave Kronos the stone to swallow.

492-493 It seems to take a year for Zeus to grow up; the length of time may reflect the
    role of the Minoan year-god.

494-496 "Clever advice of Gaia" may be what she told Rhea, or may now tell Zeus.
    Apollodoros (1.2.1) says Metis assisted Zeus by giving Kronos an emetic drug.

497-500 The stone disgorged by Kronos was exhibited at Delphi (Pytho), where
    Pausanias saw it (10.24). Parnassos is the mountain of Delphi, and Pytho, at first
    the general area around Delphi, became an alternate name for Delphi itself. There
    was a more famous stone at Delphi, the *omphalos* [navel-stone] which marked Del-
    phi as the center of the earth. Pausanias (10.16) distinguishes the *omphalos* from
    the stone of Kronos, but Pausanias is almost 900 years later than Hesiod, who per-
    haps identifies the two.

501-506 The "uncles" (501) must be the Kyklopes, who were imprisoned in Tartaros
    by Ouranos and who will give Zeus the lightning (504-505); the freeing of their
    brothers, the Hundred-Handed, will be reported in 617-626. The Greek text is am-
    bivalent on whether the "father" in 502 is Ouranos or Kronos; Hesiod must have
    meant Ouranos, but Apollodoros says that Kronos released the Kyklopes and Hun-
    dred-Handed at the time of Ouranos' castration and then imprisoned them again in
    Tartaros (1.1.4-5).

and gave him thunder and the fiery lightning-bolt
and lightning, which vast Gaia earlier had hidden;   505
relying on these, he is king of mortals and immortals.
   Iapetos married the fine-ankled daughter of Okeanos,
Klymene, and went up to the same bed;°
she bore him a son, strong-hearted Atlas,° and
she bore all-eminent Menoitios, and Prometheus°   510
subtle and devious, and wrong-thinking Epimetheus,°
who was from the first an evil for men who work for food;°
he first received from Zeus the molded° woman,
the virgin. Wide-seeing Zeus sent arrogant Menoitios°
down to Erebos, striking him with a smoking thunderbolt,   515
for his recklessness and excessive pride.
And Atlas,° standing at the limits of the earth,

507-508 After hinting at Zeus' inevitable victory (506), Hesiod interrupts the story of
conflict between Zeus and his father to introduce the conflict between Zeus and
Prometheus. First, however, he must finish the account of the genealogy of the Titans; Iapetos, the one remaining Titan son, will be the father of Prometheus.
Klymene is the Okeanid of 351.

509 Atlas, the eldest of Iapetos' four sons, is the giant who holds up the sky (519).

510 Menoitios appears elsewhere only in *Ap* 1.2.3, where he is said to have been thun-
der-bolted to Tartaros during the Titanomachy. Prometheus' name was interpreted
by the Greeks to mean "Forethought," but the linguistic derivation is unclear. Some
Sanskritists associate Prometheus with the Sanskrit verb *manth*, whose primary
meaning is "vigorous backwards and forwards motion of any sort;" it refers especially to the production of fire from fire-sticks, sexual activity, stealing (particularly
the theft of ambrosia or fire), churning (see on 188-199), and it is related to the
name Mandara (the Indian mountain used for churning ambrosia/semen). The name
Prometheus might also be related to the Hindu culture-hero Prthu, who steals the
cow of immortality from the gods to help a mortal and is the founder of the civiliz-
ing arts.

511 Epimetheus [Afterthought] is the husband of Pandora and father of Pyrrha, who
marries Prometheus' son Deukalion (*Ap* 1.7.2). Deukalion and Pyrrha are the
Greek version of the Biblical Noah and his wife.

512 An allusion to Epimetheus' folly in accepting Pandora from Zeus, as described in
the following two lines.

513 Pandora is "molded," because she is made from earth by Hephaistos (571-572).

514-516 The only stated offense of the "arrogant" Menoitios is his "recklessness and
excessive pride," which must put him in the category of gigantic figures (e.g., Typhoeus, the Giants, the Aloidai) who try to usurp Zeus' position.

517-520 In the *Odyssey* (1.52-54) Atlas is the father of Kalypso and holds up the pillars which separate earth and sky. In 746-748 Atlas will be situated somewhere in
the underworld, but here he is placed with the Hesperides in their garden in the far
west. This may not be a contradiction; the location of the underworld in archaic
Greek literature is notoriously elusive, and appears in the *Theogony* as both under

before the clear-voiced Hesperides, under strong compulsion,
holds the wide sky with head and untiring arms;
or this is the fate wise Zeus allotted him.   520
He bound devious Prometheus° with inescapable
harsh bonds, fastened through the middle of a column,
and he inflicted on him a long-winged eagle, which ate
his immortal liver; but it grew as much in all
at night as the long-winged bird would eat all day.   525
Herakles,° the mighty son of fine-ankled Alkmene,
killed it and freed from evil suffering the son
of Iapetos and released him from anguish
by the will of high-ruling Olympian Zeus,

---

the earth and at the ends of the earth. The sky-holding is evidently a punishment,
since Atlas is "under strong compulsion," but the reason for his punishment is even
less clear than in the case of Menoitios. If we exclude Epimetheus, who functions
as a mortal rather than as a god (West, *T* 309-310), we are left with three similar
brothers, a "decomposition" or splitting into three versions of the figure of a rebellious giant who is punished.

521-525 Although the scene of Prometheus' punishment is said in almost all accounts
to be the Caucasus Mountains (or Skythia, which may be the same), there seems to
be another version in which he, like Atlas, is at the western ends of the earth. This
is the site of the garden of the Hesperides, and it is during Herakles' search for this
garden that he encounters Prometheus. The most famous version of Prometheus'
punishment, Aeschylus' *Prometheus Bound*, is set in Skythia (2), but in the lower
margin of the ancient Hypothesis to this play the following note appears:
"Prometheus is not bound in the Caucasus as in the usual story but at the European
limits of the ocean, as can be seen from the words spoken to Io." Aeschylus also
calls Prometheus the son of Themis (18), and an Aeschylean fragment has the eagle
visit Prometheus every other day. The focus of the eagle's attention is Prometheus'
liver, because the liver was associated with passion and erotic striving at least as
early as Aeschylus; the punishment is a kind of castration, since the offense of
Prometheus is an oedipal crime (see *Ps* 92-94). West (*T* 313-314) objects to this
significance of the liver since it is not stated explicitly before the 5th century, but it
is surely implicit in the punishment of Tityos in the *Odyssey* (11.576-579). Tityos
is bound while two vultures devour his liver, and the similarity of the punishments
inflicted on Tityos and Prometheus would suggest that the meanings of their crimes
are also similar.

526-534 Herakles, the greatest hero of Greek myth, is the son of Zeus and Alkmene.
He is usually said to have released Prometheus during his eleventh labor (the gold-
en apples of the Hesperides). There may seem to be a contradiction between this
account of Herakles' killing the eagle and freeing Prometheus "from evil suffering"
and the later statement that "great bondage holds" Prometheus (616). West (*T* 313)
takes the present tense of "holds" too literally and solves the contradiction by having Herakles kill the eagle but leave Prometheus still chained. This is possible but
unlikely; Zeus is said to have ended his anger (533), and the present tense "holds"
occurs in a moralizing coda finishing the story with a general principle.

so that the glory of Theban-born Herakles   530
would be more than before on the nurturing earth;
thinking of this, he honored his famous son, and
though he was angry quit the rage he had ever since
the Titan matched wits with Kronos' mighty son.
For when gods and mortal men made a settlement°   535
at Mekone,° then he cleverly cut up a big ox and
set it before them, trying to deceive the mind of Zeus.
For Zeus he set out meat and innards rich with fat
on the skin, covering it with the stomach of the ox;
but for men he set the white ox-bones,° with crafty skill   540
arranging them well and covering them with shining fat.

535-564 The account of the deceptive banquet at Mekone is, on one level, an explanation of why, in Greek blood sacrifice, the bones of the sacrificed animal are given
to the gods while the flesh is kept for humans to eat. Human sacrificers could justify this distribution by referring to the choice Zeus had made (knowingly, according to Hesiod) at Mekone. On another level, it is an example of a repeated motif in
the Prometheus myth, his deception of Zeus and the appropriation of Zeus' prerogative. This motif appears again in the theft of fire (565-566) and in various later
stories (e.g., that Prometheus, when creating mankind, was supposed to present his
work to Zeus for approval, but kept back and hid Phainon, the handsomest boy).
On this second level, the banquet at Mekone is parallel to the banquet of Tantalos,
who tried to deceive Zeus by serving him his chopped-up son Pelops at a meal
(Pindar, *Olympian* 1). The myths of Tantalos and Prometheus are in several ways
doubles of one another: a) at a communal meal each of them conceals something
beneath the surface of food in an ambiguously successful attempt to deceive Zeus;
b) each of them steals a prerogative of Zeus which mortals are forbidden to possess, Prometheus fire and Tantalos ambrosia (which are symbolically and structurally equivalent); c) each of them is punished by Zeus, Tantalos in Tartaros and
Prometheus in a fashion almost exactly the same as Tantalos' fellow-sufferer
Tityos. For a discussion of this comparison see *Ps* 92-94.

535-536 The meeting between men and gods at Mekone marks the end of the time
when men and gods lived and ate together; the period before their separation may
be the time of Hesiod's Golden Race (*WD* 109-126). The banquet of Tantalos, as
well as his theft of ambrosia, must also take place at a time when men and gods
have not yet been finally separated. Mekone is the old name for Sikyon, a city near
Corinth in the north-east Peloponnese.

540-541 The skillful arrangement of the bones may express the care Prometheus took
to conceal his trick from Zeus. But it may reflect the wide-spread care given to the
arrangement of bones in primitive sacrificial cults, a concern based on the hope that
the dead animal will come to life again. In a Magyar myth cited by Frazer (*Spirits
of the Corn and of the Wild* [London 1890], vol. 2, p. 263), a hero is cut into pieces;
the serpent-king lays the bones together in their proper order and washes them; the
hero comes to life, but his shoulder blade has been lost, so he is given a substitute
of gold and ivory. In the myth of Tantalos' banquet, his son Pelops is restored to
life and given an ivory shoulder to replace the shoulder Demeter had eaten.

Then the father of men and gods said to him:
"Son of Iapetos, distinguished of all gods,
sir, how unjustly you divided the portions."° 544
Thus Zeus, knowing deathless plans, spoke and mocked him.
But clever Prometheus answered him, gently
smiling, and did not forget his crafty trick:
"Zeus, most honored and greatest of eternal gods,
take of these whichever the spirit within tells you."
He spoke with the trick in mind; but Zeus, knowing deathless 550
plans, knew and did not miss the trick;° in his heart
he foresaw evils° which were going to happen to mortal men.
With both hands he lifted up the white fat,
but he was angry in mind and rage came to his spirit,
when he saw the white ox-bones in the crafty trick. 555
Therefore the tribes of men on earth burn to the
immortals white bones on reeking altars.
Greatly angry, cloud-gatherer Zeus said to him:
"Son of Iapetos, knowing thoughts beyond all,°
sir, you still have not forgotten your crafty trick." 560
So spoke angry Zeus, who knows deathless plans;
from then on, never forgetting the trick, he would
not give the strength of untiring fire to ash-trees
for mortal men, who live on the earth.°

543-544 An ironic statement, if Zeus really recognizes the trick of Prometheus (551).

550-551 "It has long been recognized that in the original story Zeus did not see through the trick and was thoroughly deceived" (West, *T* 321). Hesiod's version is an attempt to rescue Zeus, the hero of his poem, from the appearance of being duped.

552 The "evils" are the withholding of fire and the creation of Pandora.

558-559 These lines will be repeated almost exactly in *WD* 53-54.

562-564 It is unclear whether men had fire before and Zeus now deprives them of it, or if they had never possessed it. The reference to "ash-trees" (563) may refer to a belief that originally fire was present within trees (West, *T* 325); such a belief no doubt goes back to a time when fire was procured from lightning-struck trees. Alternatively, the word "ash-trees" [*melieisi*] may be an adjective with "mortal men"; in WD 143-145 the men of the Bronze Race are made from ash-trees [*melian*], and the phrase in the *Theogony* may mean "early men."

565-567 Myths of the theft of fire are found among primitive cultures on every inhabited continent. Sometimes the thief is a culture-hero like Prometheus, but typically it is an animal, most often a bird or insect (because of their ability to fly from earth to sky and back); an interesting collection of these myths is in Frazer's *Apollodorus: The Library* (Harvard 1921), vol. 2, pp. 326-350. Because of the necessity of fire for many of the technical advances of civilization, the thief of fire may become a culture-hero like Prometheus, who is said by Aeschylus to have taught men

But the great son of Iapetos deceived him°   565
and stole the far-seen light of untiring fire
in a hollow narthex;° this bit deep in the spirit
of high-thundering Zeus and his heart was angry
when he saw the far-seen light of fire among men.
In return for fire, he quickly made an evil for men;°   570
for the famous Lame One° made from earth the likeness

---

woodworking, astronomy, mathematics, the domestication of animals, navigation, medicine, prophecy, and metallurgy, in addition to giving them fire and "blind hopes" (*Prometheus Bound* 436-506). Indo-European myths contain a vast complex of stories in which fire or ambrosia is stolen from the gods and carried through the air to men; in Hindu myths, which contain the most extensive versions of this theft, fire and ambrosia are virtually interchangeable, and in Greek myth we have seen the close similarity between Prometheus (fire) and Tantalos (ambrosia). As the prerogative of the sky-god, fire ultimately represents his jealously-guarded sexual power, and the hero who steals it from him must pay for his crime with a symbolic castration. Thus the fire-god Hephaistos, defeated when he fights with Zeus on his mother's behalf, falls from sky to earth and is lamed as a result. Similarly, Frazer's collection (337-338) contains a myth of the Nigerian Ekoi in which the boy who steals fire from the Sky God is lamed as punishment; he is known only as "Lame Boy," just as Hephaistos is often referred to simply as the "Lame One" (e.g., *Th* 579). Even the animal versions contain symbolic castrations: the Karok Indians of California say that the frog originally had a tail, but lost it while stealing fire (343), and a similar story about how the deer lost its once-long tail is told by the Tlingit Indians of Alaska (348). On the psychology of the theft of fire see *Ps* 92-94.

567 A narthex is the giant fennel plant; its slowly combustible interior and hard rind make it an appropriate vessel in which to carry and conceal fire.

570-589 Zeus punishes men by ordering the creation and adornment of Pandora, the first woman. How men earlier reproduced themselves without women is not mentioned, but belief in some sort of asexual reproduction is not impossible. Myths told of men being born from stones (*Ap* 1.7.2) or from the earth, through the work of a craftsman god like Prometheus or Hephaistos; both Prometheus and Hephaistos are called the creators of Pandora, and Prometheus is said to have created men from earth and water (*Ap* 1.7.1) just as Hephaistos made Pandora (*WD* 60-61). Within a few centuries of Hesiod's time the first Greek philosophers were repeating these ideas in a new form of "scientific" speculation. For Anaximander, life began when water and earth were heated to a certain temperature; since this took place in the "moist," the first men during the helplessness of infancy were nurtured and reared within fish. In the 5th century Archelaus of Athens is supposed to have believed that at first men appeared from the earth, were nurtured on ooze, and only later began to reproduce, Empedokles said that "shoots of miserable men and women" were born "from the earth, having a portion both of water and heat," and Demokritos held that the first men were created from water and mud (these theories are discussed W. K. C. Guthrie, *In the Beginning* [Ithaca 1957] 32-38).

571-572 The "Lame One" is Hephaistos. These two lines are repeated almost exactly in *WD* 70-71; earlier in the latter poem Hephaistos is ordered by Zeus to make Pandora from earth and water (60-61).

of a modest virgin, by the plans of Kronos' son.
Owl-eyed Athena sashed her and dressed her°
in silver clothes; she placed with her hands a
decorated veil on her head, marvelous to see;   575
[and lovely fresh garlands, the flowers of plants,
Pallas Athene put around her head]°
and she placed on her head a golden crown
which the famous Lame One had made himself,
shaping it with his hands, to please father Zeus.   580
On it he carved many designs, a marvelous sight;
of all dread beasts the land and sea nourish,
he included most, amazingly similar to living
animals with voices; and beauty breathed over all.

    But when he made the lovely evil to pay for the good,   585
he led her where the other gods and men were;°
she delighted in the finery from the great father's
owl-eyed daughter; awe filled immortal gods and mortal
men when they saw the sheer trick, irresistible to men.
For from her is the race of female women,°   590
[from her is the deadly race and tribes of women]°

---

573 This line reappears as WD 72. Athena and Hephaistos, the two gods most closely
associated with crafts, are entrusted with the creation, dressing, and adornment of
Pandora. In *WD* 60-82 a divine task force joins in this work, including Hephaistos
(60), Athena (63), Aphrodite (65), Hermes (67), the Charites [Graces] and Peitho
[Persuasion] (73), and the Horai [Seasons] (75). In addition to an elaborate adornment scene, the *WD* version adds other details not found in the *Theogony*: the name
Pandora is given to the woman (who is unnamed in the *Theogony*) because all the
gods "presented a gift" (82), which probably means that all the gods gave Pandora
as a gift to men, not that each god gave her a separate gift; Pandora is received by
Epimetheus, despite Prometheus' warning never to take a gift from Zeus (84-89);
Pandora opens a jar and allows all evils and diseases to escape into the world, while
retaining Elpis [Hope] within the jar (94-104); before Pandora and her jar men
lived a paradisal existence (90-92) like that of the Golden Race (109-120).

576-577 These lines are suspected by most editors because of the repetition of
Athena's name in 573 and 577.

586 If before Pandora mankind lived in a Golden Age, this would explain why men
and gods are together when Pandora is brought out for exhibition (see on 535-536).

590-601 The *Theogony* version is much more misogynistic that the *WD* version. In the
latter the evils come from the jar which Pandora unfortunately opens, but here it is
woman herself who is a great evil to man. This evil, it turns out, is the old-age complaint (of envious men) that women are idle consumers of the wealth a man has
worked hard to amass.

591 Since 590 and 591 are alternate expressions, one of the lines is presumably not
genuine.

a great plague to mortals, dwelling with men,
not suited for cursed Poverty, but for Wealth.°
As when bees in covered hives feed°
the drones, companions of evil works,   595
the bees work until sunset, all day
and every day, and make the pale combs,
while the drones stay inside, in the covered hives,
reaping the work of others into their own stomachs;
similarly for mortal men, high-thundering Zeus·   600
made an evil: women, the partners of evil works.
He gave a second evil to balance a good,°
since whoever escapes marriage and women's harm,
by refusing to marry, comes to deadly old age
with no son to tend him; not lacking livelihood   605
while he lives, when he dies distant kin divide
his estate. But° even the man whose fate is to marry
and acquires a good wife, suited to his wants,
for him from the first good and evil are balanced
always; but whoever acquires the wicked sort   610
lives with unending trouble in his mind and
spirit and heart, and the evil is incurable.
So it is impossible to cheat or surpass the mind of Zeus.
For not even Iapetos' son, good Prometheus,
escaped his heavy anger, but of necessity   615
great bondage holds him, though he knows many things.°

---

593 Poverty [Penia] and Wealth [Koros] are personified; they have no role in myth, although Plato makes Penia the mother of Eros (*Symposium* 203b).

594-601 A bee and drone simile recurs in *WD* 303-306, where a man who does not work is compared to the idle drones:

> Gods and men are angry at a man who lives
> without work, behaving like the stingless drones
> who waste the bees' labor, not working but eating

602-607 The "second evil" (602) is lack of a son (605), and the "good" (602) is managing to escape marriage and to live alone. If someone avoids the first evil (woman) by remaining single, he will receive the second evil from Zeus, the absence of a son to take care of him in his old age and maintain his estate after he has died.

607-612 It is impossible, even for the man who manages to find a good wife, to have unmixed happiness, but the man who marries a bad wife will have unmixed misery. Why will the man with a good wife have evil as well as good? This may refer to the evils and diseases released from Pandora's jar in the WD, but it may also mean that even the good wife is not altogether good (see *Ps* 103).

616 For the apparent discrepancy between Prometheus' present bondage and his earlier liberation by Herakles, see on 526-534.

When first the father was angry at heart with Obriareos°
and Kottos and Gyges, he bound them in strong bondage;
when he noticed their great manhood, their looks
and size, he put them under the wide-pathed earth.°   620
They lived there under the earth in pain,
at the farthest borders of the great earth,°
suffering much and long, with great grief of heart.
But Kronos' son and the other immortal gods,
whom fair-haired Rhea bore from Kronos' embrace,   625
brought them up to the light, by Gaia's counsel.
For she told them everything° in detail, how with
their help they would win victory and bright fame.
For a long time they fought in bitter exertion
against one another in harsh battles,   630
the Titan gods and those born of Kronos,

617-620 The digression on Prometheus and the creation of woman has completed the
genealogies of the Titans, and Hesiod returns to the war between the Olympians
and the Titans (the Titanomachy), which was about to begin at 506. Myths world-
wide contain stories of a war between the gods at the beginning (or end) of the
world. The most relevant parallel to the Greek Titanomachy is the Babylonian
"Enuma Elish," in which Marduk, like Zeus, defeats the older generation of gods
(*In* 22-23).

Obriareos is a lengthened form of Briareos, one of the Hundred-Handed; Homer
(*Iliad* 1.404) says that the gods call him Briareos, but men call him Aigaion.
Having already released the Kyklopes and acquired a lightning supply (501-506),
Zeus releases the three Hundred-Handed, who will be his heavy artillery. The
Hundred-Handed will play a large role in the war (only they and Zeus are
mentioned as fighting on the Olympian side), while the Kyklopes disappear from
view, their lightning now in the hands of Zeus.

Who is the "father" in 617, Ouranos or Kronos? West (*T* 338) believes that it is
"obviously" Ouranos, but how could Ouranos have noticed (and envied) their
"manhood, their looks and size" if he did not allow them out of their mother's body
(156-158)? Either the "father" is Kronos (as in *Ap* 1.1.5) or (and this may be more
likely) the "manhood,etc." of the Hundred-Handed is a result of the projective envy
of Ouranos, the very reason for which he keeps them from being born.

622 Earth's "farthest borders" may be the farthest down (i.e., Tartaros), or the phrase
may be equivalent to such expressions as "beyond Okeanos." Atlas also is located
both in the far west and in the underworld (see on 517-520), and Homer situates the
underworld itself "beyond Okeanos," "far under the earth," and "at the limits of the
earth."

626-628 Gaia prophesies that the Olympians will win the war if they secure the help of
the Hundred-Handed. In the war of the Olympian gods against the Giants (*Ap*
1.6.1), the gods possess an oracle revealing that the Giants can only be killed if the
gods have a mortal ally; Gaia, who is on the opposite side in this war, tries to help

the proud Titans from lofty Othrys
and from Olympos° the gods, givers of good,
whom fair-haired Rhea bore, having lain with Kronos.
With bitter war against one another   635
they fought continually for ten full years;°
there was no end or relief from harsh strife
for either, the war's outcome was evenly balanced.
But when he gave them everything fitting,°
nectar and ambrosia, which the gods eat themselves,   640
and the proud spirit grew in the breasts of all,
[when they tasted nectar and desirable ambrosia]
then the father of gods and men said to them:
     "Hear me, good children of Gaia and Ouranos,
that I may say what the spirit in my chest commands.°   645
For a long time now against one another
we have fought every day for victory and power,
the Titan gods and we born of Kronos.
Show your great strength and unbeatable arms
against the Titans in savage war;   650
remember our kindness, and how much you suffered
before you came to the light from grievous bondage
under the murky gloom, thanks to our plans."
     When he had spoken, blameless Kottos replied:
     "Divine one, you tell us what we know; on our own   655
we know your superior mind and thoughts, and
that you defended the immortals from icy harm;

the Giants by searching for an herbal drug to make the Giants invulnerable to mortals, but Zeus finds the herb first and picks it.

632-633 The "Olympian" gods first acquire this title because Mount Olympos is the site of their camp in the war. Since Olympos is north of the Thessalian plain and Mount Othrys, the Titans' camp, is south of the plain, the battle itself was presumably fought on the plain between the two mountains.

636 We learn now that the war has already lasted for ten years when Zeus learns from Gaia of the need for the Hundred-Handed. The Trojan War also lasts for ten years; see on 722-725.

639-641 After their long stay in the underworld, the Hundred-Handed are revived by eating ambrosia and nectar. For ambrosia see on 510 and *Ps* 93; nectar is usually the liquid counterpart of ambrosia, but the two foods are frequently indistinguishable. The divine meal enables the Hundred-Handed to fight and also, it seems, to talk, just as Odysseus gives a drink of blood to the spirits of the dead so they will converse with him (*Odyssey* 11).

645 The appearance of this line nine times in the Homeric poems is a good example not of one poet borrowing from another, but of the shared repertory of epic singers.

by your counsels we came back from the murky gloom,
back from the unyielding bonds, obtaining
the unexpected, lord son of Kronos.   660
So now with firm mind and willing spirit
we will defend your power in hostile war,
fighting the Titans in harsh battles."
　　After he spoke, the gods who give good welcomed
the words they heard; their spirit longed for war   665
even more than before, and they roused grim conflict
that same day, all of them, female as well as male,°
the Titan gods against those born of Kronos and
those Zeus brought to light from darkness
under the earth, dread and strong, with huge might.   670
A hundred arms shot from the shoulders
of each and all, fifty heads grew from the
shoulders of each, from their massive bodies.
They stood against the Titans in grim battle,
holding great rocks in their massive hands;   675
the Titans opposite strengthened their ranks
expectantly; both displayed the work of arms
and might together, and the vast sea echoed loudly
and the earth resounded greatly, and the wide sky
shook and groaned, and great Olympos was shaken   680
from its foundation by the immortals' charge; a heavy
tremor of feet reached dim Tartaros, and the loud
noise of unspeakable rout and violent weapons.
So they hurled at each other the painful weapons;°
shouts from both sides reached starry Ouranos,   685
as they came together with a great outcry.
　　Zeus no longer restrained his might, but now his
heart was filled with wrath, and he revealed all
his strength; from the sky and Olympos both,
he came throwing a lightning-flurry; the bolts   690
flew thick with thunder and lightning
from his massive hand, whirling a holy flame,

---

667 Even the goddesses take part in the war, although Hesiod is silent about their role. In the war against the Giants, none of Zeus' sisters participate, although Artemis kills Aigaion (the Homeric name for one of the Hundred-Handed [see on 617-620]), Athena throws an island on Enkelados, and the Moirai club two Giants to death (*Ap* 1.6.2).

684 What weapons the Titans hurled is unknown.

one after another; the life-giving earth resounded
in flames, the vast woods crackled loudly about,
the whole earth and Okeanos' streams and the   695
barren sea were boiling; the hot blast enveloped
the chthonic° Titans, the flame reached the upper
air in its fury; although they were strong, the blazing
glow of thunder and lightning blinded their eyes.
The awful heat seized Chaos;° it seemed,   700
for eyes to see and ears to hear the sound,
just as if earth and wide sky from above came
together; for so great a noise would arise
from the one fallen upon and the other falling down;
such a noise arose from the strife of clashing gods.   705
The winds° stirred up earthquake and dust and
thunder and lighting and blazing lightning-bolt,
the weapons of great Zeus, and brought the shout
and cry into the midst of both sides; a great din
arose from fearful strife, and might's work was revealed.   710
    But the tide of battle turned; before, in mutual
collision, they fought continuously in grim battles;
but now in the front ranks they° roused dread war,
Kottos and Briareos and Gyges, hungry for war.
They threw three hundred rocks from massive hands   715
at once, and with their missiles overshadowed
the Titans; they sent them under the wide-pathed
earth, and bound them in cruel bonds,
having defeated them by force, despite their daring,
as far below the earth as sky is above the earth;°   720

---

697 The Titans are called "chthonic" [chthonious] because their mother is Earth
(*chthon* = earth]; see on 767.

700 Chaos is mentioned not because we are expected to know the exact location of the
first being, but to indicate the enormous space which felt the blast of heat. Chaos is
somewhere in the underworld (814), and presumably far below the surface of the
earth; the heat extends even down to Chaos, just as it reaches up to the "upper air"
[*aither*, 697].

706-709 The winds do not cause earthquake, lightning, etc., but amplify their effect.
Winds also play an important role in Marduk's battle against Titmat and the older
gods in the "Enuma Elish" (*In* 22-23).

713-719 Now that Zeus seems to have won the war, the HUndred-Handed are re-intro-
duced to finish the job and to fulfill Gaia's prophecy (626-628).

720-819) That the description of the underworld takes up exactly 100 lines is probably
not meaningful, since no editor regards all of the lines as genuine (West brackets
734-745, 768, and 774). Hesiod's underworld can be reconstructed only in a very

for it is that far from the earth to dim Tartaros.°
    A bronze anvil falling for nine nights and days
from the sky would reach the earth on the tenth;°
and a bronze anvil falling for nine nights and days
from the earth would reach Tartaros on the tenth.   725
Around it runs a bronze fence;° and about its
neck flows night° in a triple row; while above
grow the roots° of earth and the barren sea.

---

general sense; many details are uncertain or contradictory, including the important
question whether Tartaros is the entire underworld or only its lowest part. The surface of Tartaros lies as far below the surface of the earth as the earth below the sky,
with an open space between (open enough, at any rate, for an anvil to fall for ten
days); night "flows" around it, and the "roots" of earth and sea are above it (720-
728). In 743, however, the sources (= roots?) of earth, sea, sky, and Tartaros are all
together (in Tartaros?) and a man entering the open space would fall, or be blown
around by winds, for at least a year before reaching the bottom. "In front" (of Tartaros?) are Atlas (746) and the homes of Night and Day (748); Sleep and Death
(758-759), Hades (767), Kerberos (769), and Styx (776). The four lines about the
sources of earth, sea, sky, and Tartaros (736-739) are then repeated exactly in a
supposedly genuine passage (807-810), and the open space between earth and Tartaros seems to be identified as Chaos (814). But earlier, in 729-731, it seemed that
earth included this open space and perhaps Tartaros as well, since the Titans are
imprisoned at the "limits of vast earth." The Hundred-Handed are the guards of
Tartaros (734-735), but also live at the foundations of Okeanos (815-816). We
should assume, I think, that the underworld is everything below the earth's surface,
that Tartaros is Hesiod's name for the underworld, that the Titans are put in a
prison at the farthest point of Tartaros, that Hades, Night, Styx, etc., are outside the
prison but inside Tartaros, that the roots, or sources, of the four cosmological divi-
sions are in Tartaros (that is, they all reach beneath the earth's surface), that even
Chaos is located in Tartaros, and that at certain points (especially the far west beyond Okeanos) the limits of the earth extend horizontally as well as vertically. In
later Greek thought, the prison itself is called Tartaros and receives new inhabitants, and the entire underworld comes to be called Hades.

720-721 For Homer Tartaros is as far below "Hades' house" as earth is below sky (Iliad 8.16).

722-725 The number ten seems to be a popular choice for mythic expressions of great
magnitude or duration. The anvil falls for nine days and lands on the tenth, the Titan-War and Trojan War last for ten years apiece, and the prophet Teiresias, asked
whether men or women get greater pleasure in sex, answers that on a scale of ten
men are one and women are nine (Ap 3.6.7). See also on 789-792, 801-804, 918-
920. Any discussion of the significance of the number ten and the ratio 9:1 should
bear in mind that by the Greek method of reckoning time a child is born in the tenth
month of its mother's pregnancy (e.g., Hh to Hermes 11: Hermes is born in the
"tenth moon").

726 The fence establishes the location of the Titans as a prison.

727 "Night" may signify here the darkness of Chaos (814).

728 The "roots" of earth and sea are their lowest extensions (see on 807-810). The notion of a "world-tree" appears in the cosmological myths of many cultures, and is

There the Titan gods under the dim gloom
are hid away by the plans of cloud-gatherer Zeus, 730
in a moldy place, the limits of vast earth.°
For them is no escape, since Poseidon put in
bronze doors,° and the fence runs on both sides.
[There Gyges, Kottos, and great-spirited Obriareos
live, the faithful guards of Zeus Aigiochos.]° 735
There dark earth and dim Tartaros
and the barren sea and starry sky
all have their sources and limits in a row,
terrible and dank, which even the gods abhor;°
[the chasm is great, and not until a year's end° 740
would a man reach the bottom, if first he were within
the doors, but terrible gust after gust would carry him
here and there; it is awful even for the immortal gods]
[this is monstrous; and the terrible house
of dim Nyx stands covered in dark clouds] 745
In front the son of Iapetos° holds the wide sky
with his head and untiring arms, standing
immobile, where Nyx and Hemera° come near and
address one another, passing the great threshold
of bronze; one will go down in, the other comes from 750
the door, and the house never holds both within,
but always one is out of the house and
traverses the earth, while the other is in the house
and awaits the time of her journey, when it will come;

especially prominent among the northern Indo-Europeans (e.g., Celtic, Norse, Siberian), but is absent from Hesiod's cosmology.

731 See on 720-819.

732-733 Of the three sons of Kronos, only Poseidon is associated with building.

734-735 These lines are bracketed because they seem contradicted at 815-819 (West, *T* 358), but the two passages may express the same notion in different forms.

736-739 See on 807-810.

740-743 These lines are bracketed because they seem to contradict 724-725 (West, *T* 364). West's arguments here are problematic; Hesiod does not portray the chasm as bottomless (as West maintains), and the time difference between anvils and a man may be due to the effect of the "terrible" gusts of wind rather than the difference in weight between a man and an anvil.

746-747 The son of Iapetos is Atlas; "in front" here as in 767 means apart from the prison of the Titans. Ubelluri, the Hurrian Atlas in the "Song of Ullikummi," seems to live beneath the sea (*In* 26).

748-754 Night and Day live in the same house beneath the earth, but never at the same time.

one holds much-seeing light° for those on earth,   755
the other,° who holds in her arms Hypnos, brother of
Thanatos, is deadly Nyx, covered in misty cloud.
    There the children of dark Nyx have their homes,
Hypnos and Thanatos, awful gods; never does
shining Helios look on them with his beams,   760
as he goes up to the sky or comes down from the sky.
The former crosses the earth and wide backs of
the sea harmless and gentle to men, but the
other's heart is iron, and his bronze heart is
pitiless in his chest; he holds whomever he once   765
seizes of men; he is hateful even to the immortal gods.
    There in front the echoing homes of the nether° god
[of mighty Hades and awesome Persephone]°
stand, and a terrible dog° is on guard in front,
unpitying possessor of an evil trick; on those   770
going in he fawns with his tail and both ears, but
does not let them go back out and, waiting,
eats whomever he catches going out the doors.
[of mighty Hades and awesome Persephone]°
    There dwells a goddess° hated by the immortals,   775
terrible Styx, eldest daughter of back-flowing
Okeanos; away from the gods she lives in a noble
house, roofed with great rocks; on all sides

---

755 "Much-seeing light" is not the sun, but the light of day.

756-766 Night's children Hypnos [Sleep] and Death [Thanatos], since they are never seen by Helios [Sun], seem to have their effect on mortals only at night, when they are carried abroad in their mother's arms. This poetic expression surely does not mean that mortals can die or sleep only at night, but it may imply that Death comes to claim his due at night (perhaps after burial; in Euripides' Alcestis, Death is not present when Alkestis dies, but is found later by Herakles at her tomb). Did ancient Greeks sleep during the day, and if they did was it out of the sunlight?

767 The word translated "nether" is chthoniou, which here must mean "under the earth's surface"; see on 697. The "nether god" is Hades.

768 This line is bracketed because it seems redundant (and therefore may be a clarification added later).

769-773 The dog of Hades is Kerberos; see on 310-312.

774 This line repeats 768.

775-779 For Styx, see 383-401 and notes on 399, 412, 421-425; that Styx is hated [*stygere*] is implied in her name [*Styg-*]. Okeanos is called "back-flowing" because he circles the earth and flows back into himself. The columns which reach up to the sky are reminiscent of the "sources" of the sky which extend into the underworld (777-778), and both concepts are most easily understood if we imagine the underworld as extending to the "limits" of the earth's surface as well as of its depth (see following note).

it reaches up to the sky with silver pillars.
Rarely does Iris,° swift-footed daughter of Thaumas,   780
come as messenger over the sea's wide backs.
Whenever conflict and strife arise among the immortals°
and one of those who have Olympian homes should lie,
Zeus sends Iris to bring the gods' great oath
from afar in a golden pitcher, the famous cold   785
water which trickles down from a high steep
rock; far below the wide-pathed earth it
flows from the holy river° through black night;
a branch of Okeanos, a tenth part° is allotted to it;
nine parts winding around the earth and sea's wide   790
backs in silver eddies fall into the sea, but the
tenth flows out from the rock, a great woe to the gods.
Whoever pours libation and breaks his oath,° of the
immortals who hold the peaks of snowy Olympos,
lies unbreathing until the year's end;   795
he never comes near ambrosia and nectar
for food, but lies unbreathing and unspeaking
on a covered bed, and an evil coma covers him.
But when he ends being sick for a great year,°
another harsher ordeal succeeds the first;   800
for nine years he is parted from the gods who always

780-781 For Iris as messenger, see on 266. That Iris must travel across the sea to reach
   Styx suggests again that the underworld (or its entrance) is located, at least in part,
   at the farthest limits of the earth's surface.
782-784 Styx was appointed the gods' oath at 400. By pouring a libation consisting of
   the water of Styx (793), a god commits himself to the punishment described in 795-
   803 if he should swear falsely. 783-784 might seem to imply that an oath is sworn
   only after a god is detected lying, which would make the oath superfluous. What
   they must mean is that in a dispute between the gods, one of the disputing parties
   must be lying, but it is not known which one. They therefore swear an oath by
   Styx, and the liar (if found out), or the one who does not do what he promises, is
   punished.
788 The "holy river" is Okeanos (789).
789-792 A tenth part of Okeanos' water flows down through the earth, emerging as a
   waterfall down from a high rock. Again we have the number ten and the ratio 9:1
   (see on 722-725).
793-798 Whether the coma is the result or cause of ambrosia-deprivation is not made
   clear.
799-804 The one-year coma of the perjuring god is followed by nine years of solitary
   banishment from the company of the other gods, which ends "in the tenth" (803).
   Again the number ten and the 9:1 ratio. I know of no instance in which a god is
   said to have undergone this punishment.

are, and never joins in council and feasts,
for nine full years; in the tenth he rejoins the
meetings of the immortals who have Olympian homes.
The gods made the eternal and primal water of Styx°   805
such an oath; it emerges through a forbidding place.
    There dark earth and dim Tartaros°
and the barren sea and starry sky
all have their sources and limits in a row,
terrible and dank, which even the gods abhor.   810
There are shining gates and a bronze threshold°
with never-ending roots, unmoveable and
natural; beyond and far from all the gods
live the Titans, past gloomy Chaos.°
But the famous helpers of loud-thundering Zeus°   815
live in houses on Okeanos' foundations,
Kottos and Gyges; but the deep-roaring Earth-Shaker
made Briareos his son-in-law for his courage,
and gave him his daughter Kymopoleia to marry.
    But when Zeus drove the Titans from the sky,°   820

---

805 The water of Styx is immortal because the goddess Styx is immortal. In much later myths the immortality of this water could be transferred to someone (e.g., Achilleus) who was dipped in it (Hyginus, *Fabula* 107).

807-810 Earth, Tartaros, sea, and sky are the four components of the universe. Their "sources and limits" are presumably the same as the "roots" in 728. That they are "in a row" [hexeies] probably means that they are separate, at least at some point. The "roots" of earth and sea were said to be above the prison of the Titans (727-728); perhaps the roots of Tartaros are below those of earth and sea, and those of sky are above.

811-814 The gates and threshold are those of the entrance to the underworld. In a sense, they are the most important part of the underworld, the entrance which allows no exit. The most famous version of this gate is the door in Canto 3 of Dante's *Inferno*, above which is a sign ending "Abandon all hope, you who enter here." Through Dante's door one encounters first the river Acheron and its ferryman Charon; on the far side is a bottomless Abyss (like Chaos); the Styx, portrayed as a waterfall ending in a great swamp, appears in Canto 7.

814 Chaos seems to be an open space between Tartaros and the earth's surface (see on 720-819).

815-819 Briareos is singled out from his brother Hundred-Handed to marry Poseidon's daughter, but he still may live with his brothers. Their homes "on Okeanos' foundations" seem to be among the roots, limits, and sources in the underworld; this passage does not necessarily contradict 734-735.

820-868 Zeus must now fight one last battle before he can settle down to the business of ruling and procreating. Angered by the defeat of the Titans, Gaia mates with Tartaros (see on 822) and produces Typhoeus, the most formidable monster of

vast Gaia bore her youngest child Typhoeus
from the love of Tartaros, through golden Aphrodite;°
his hands are strong, to do his work, and the   *Zeus does ttce?*
mighty god's legs never tire; from his shoulders
grew a hundred snake-heads, a dread serpent's°   825
with dark and lambent tongues; his eyes
under the brows on the awesome heads shot fire;
[from all the heads fire blazed as he glowered]°
from all the dread heads came voices° which
spoke all unspeakable sounds; at one time,   830
they made sounds the gods understand; at another,
the sound of a proud bellowing bull, unstoppable
in wrath; at another, a lion with ruthless spirit;
again, sounds like a pack of dogs, marvelous to hear;
again, he would hiss and high mountains re-echoed.   835

---

them all. In later accounts, the war between Zeus and Typhoeus is more complicated and of less certain outcome than in Hesiod's version; Apollodoros has Typhoeus temporarily win the upper hand by cutting out the sinews of Zeus' feet and
hands and hiding them (1.6.3), and Nonnos (5th century A.D.) has Typhoeus steal
Zeus' thunder and lightning, as well as the sinews (Dionysiaka 1). For Hesiod,
however, the battle is decided as soon as Zeus exerts his full power (853-855), just
as he had won the Titanomachy by throwing off restraint and attacking in full force
(687-689). The Typhoeus-War, in fact, is very much a repetition of the Titan-War,
and Typhoeus will end up in Tartaros with the Titans. The Typhoeus episode has
obvious parallels with Near Eastern myth (West, *T* 21-22, 379-380, 391-392), especially the Hurrian "Song of Ullikummi," in which the Storm-God becomes king but
must then fight against the giant diorite monster Ullikummi (*In* 25). For the relationship between Typhoeus and Hephaistos, and the psychological meaning of this
episode, see *Ps* 100-102.

822 This line could be excised without damage to the text. Tartaros is personified no-
where else in the *Theogony*, Typhoeus is a parthenogenic son (of Hera) in *Hh to
Apollo* 305-356 (see *Ps* 100-102), and Gaia, in a parallel incident, produces the Giants quasi-parthenogenically (their father is the blood of Ouranos, *Th* 183-186) because of her anger at the defeat of the Titans (*Ap* 1.6.1).

825 Typhoeus is part serpent, like his mate Echidna (297-307), and he has multiple
heads, like his children Orthos, Kerberos, Hydra, and Chimaira (309-322).

828 This line seems redundant.

829-835 The different sounds made by Typhoeus may suggest that separate heads had
the shapes of different animals, or that Typhoeus was able to metamorphize into
different animals. The first alternative appears in the mannerist epic version of
Nonnos (*Dionysiaka* 1.157-162, 2.250-257, 2.367-370), and the second associates
Typhoeus with the animal metamorphoses of Egyptian gods (e.g., Ammon/ram,
Horus/hawk, Osiris/goat, Isis/cow, Thoth/ibis). Typhoeus was identified by the 5th
century with the Egyptian god Seth, the evil brother and enemy of Osiris, and Seth
could change into a variety of animal forms (West, *T* 386).

A thing past help would have happened that day
and he would have ruled over immortals and mortals,
if the king of men and gods had not thought quickly.°
He° thundered hard and strong, and all the earth
resounded horribly, and the wide sky above and   840
sea and Okeanos' streams and earth's lowest parts.
Great Olympos trembled under the immortal feet
of the lord setting out, and the earth groaned.
Heat from both of them seized the violent sea,
from thunder and lightning, from the monster's fire,   845
from searing winds° and from the fiery lightning-bolt.
The whole earth was boiling, and the sky and sea;
great waves raged around and over the coasts from
the immortals' attack, and endless rumbling arose;
Hades, lord of the dead below, trembled, and so   850
did the Titans around Kronos in Tartaros,
from the endless noise and awful war.
　　When the anger of Zeus reached its height,°
he seized his weapons, thunder and lighting and
lightning-bolt, leaped from Olympos, and struck;   855
he burned all the dread monster's unspeakable heads.°
When he had whipped him and broken him with blows,
he threw him down crippled, and great Gaia groaned.°

836-838 The intention of Typhoeus is to become king of gods and men. His role then
　　is not so much parallel to Kronos and the Titans, whom Zeus defeated in order to
　　become king, as to the hypothetical successor of Zeus, the son who may overthrow
　　Zeus and continue the pattern of the succession myth (*Ps* 100-102). Nonnos' ver-
　　sion makes clear Typhoeus' chief intention is to become the husband of Hera.
　　Nymphs throughout the world fear for their virginities when he announces the orgy
　　that will take place when he comes to power: Orion will have Artemis, and Tityos
　　will finally have Leto; Kadmos is promised his choice of Athena, Leto, Charis,
　　Aphrodite, Artemis, or Hebe, in fact anyone but Hera; and all these goddesses will
　　serve at the elaborately-described wedding Typhoeus proposes for himself and
　　Hera.
839-852 The cosmic repercussions of the battle duplicate in detail the description of
　　the Titanomachy (677-686).
853-867 Again the details of the Titanomachy are recalled: Zeus is angry and releases
　　his full strength (853-855, 687-693); the earth is set on fire (859-867, 693-700).
846 The "searing winds" recall the winds used by Marduk in the "Enuma Elish" (see
　　on 706-709).
856 Zeus does to Typhoeus what Iolaos did to Hydra (see on 313-318).
858 It is possible that "crippled" [*gyiotheis*] Typhoeus is associated with the "Lame
　　One" [*Amphigyeeis*] Hephaistos, also defeated and crippled by Zeus (*Ps* 98-100).

Fire° poured from the thunderstruck lord
in the dark rugged glens of the mountain where   860
he was hit, and the vast earth burned widely
from unspeakable heat, and melted as tin
is melted in well-bored crucibles by workmen's
skill, or as iron, hardest of all things,
is melted by burning fire in mountain glens   865
in the holy earth, by the arts of Hephaistos;
so the earth melted in the glare of blazing fire.
And Zeus, vexed in spirit, threw him into wide Tartaros.
    From Typhoeus is the strength of wet-blowing winds,°
except Notos and Boreas and clearing Zephyros;   870
these are a sort from the gods, a great help to mortals.
But the other winds blow false on the sea;
some fall upon the misty sea, a great plague
to mortals, and they rage with evil storm;
they blow unpredictably, scattering ships and   875
killing sailors; there is no defense against
their harm for men who meet them on the sea.
And other winds on the vast flowering earth
destroy the beautiful fields of earth-born men,
filling them with dust and terrible tumult.   880
    But when the blessed gods had finished their work°
and decided the matter of rights with the Titans
by force, they urged wide-seeing Olympian Zeus
to be king and rule the immortals, by Gaia's
advice; and he divided their honors among them.°   885

---

859 In later versions the fire which pours from the defeated Typhoeus becomes the
    volcanic activity of the mountain under which he is imprisoned (e.g., *Ap* 1.6.3).
869-880 The destructive winds descended from Typhoeus are connected with their fa-
    ther not in that they are "wet-blowing," but because they and he are evil. The good
    winds Notos, Boreas, and Zephyros are the sons of Astraios and Eos (378-380).
881-885 The capricious Gaia now advises the gods to make Zeus king. They comply.
885 Hesiod's brief reference to Zeus' division of the gods' honors is expressed more
    specifically and somewhat differently in *Iliad* 15.187-193, where Poseidon de-
    scribes the division of the world by lot between himself and his two brothers:
        For we are three brothers from Kronos, and Rhea bore us,
        Zeus and I, and third is Hades, who rules the dead;
        all things were divided three ways, and each has a share
        of honor; I received from the shaken lots the sea to live
        in always, Hades received the misty gloom, and

Zeus,° king of gods,° made Metis° his first wife,
she who knows most of gods and mortal men.
But when she was about to bear the owl-eyed
goddess Athena, then he deceived her mind with a
trick of wily words, and put her down in his belly,   890

Zeus received the wide sky in the clouds and clear air;
but earth and high Olympos are common to us all.

886-929 Now that Zeus is king of the gods, he turns immediately to the task that will
chiefly occupy him from now on, sex and procreation. This section of the *Theogony* lists the seven wives of Zeus and their children.

For a variety of reasons, it is generally agreed that the ending of the *Theogony*
was not written by Hesiod, but there is general disagreement as to where what
remains of the original *Theogony* ends and the later revision of the ending of the
Theogony begins. West (*T* 397-399) argues persuasively that the original ending
was similar to the ending we now have, but that everything after line 900 was
remodeled by a later poet, perhaps in the 6th century. This second poet substituted
for Hesiod's ending his own version, designed to lead into the *Catalogue of
Women*. During the Alexandrian period this long poem of "Hesiod," consisting of
the *Theogony* and the *Catalogue of Women* together, was divided into two poems
by scholars, who decided that the *Theogony* should end at line 1020. In addition to
the original ending of the *Theogony*, now lost, Hesiod may also have composed
something like the *Catalogue of Women*. The surviving fragments of the poem by
that name, however, which was usually attributed to Hesiod in antiquity, were
written not by Hesiod but by the poet who revised the ending of the *Theogony*.

886 Metis is a daughter of Okeanos (358).

886-900 Having succeeded to the position of king of the gods, Zeus is still not entirely
secure. His father and grandfather also ruled, but were deposed by their sons. Zeus
needs both strength and strategic knowledge to protect his kingship; his power was
evident in the wars with the Titans and Typhoeus, and his acquisition of knowledge
is now demonstrated, at least symbolically, in the outcome of his first marriage.
Metis has two important functions: she is destined to bear a son who will replace
Zeus as king of gods and men (897-898), and she, who "knows most" (887), is the
personification of practical wisdom [metis], the art of knowing what to do with
what one learns. Zeus exhibits his metis both practically and metaphorically: first,
by following the advice of Gaia and thereby preventing the birth of the ominous
son, and second, by swallowing Metis and thus incorporating within himself the
metis she represents. The child Metis is pregnant with when Zeus swallows her is
Athena, whose birth from Zeus' head will be recounted in 924-926. Although Hesiod implies that Zeus' strategy is sufficient, other myths present a more complicated situation. In one version Zeus learns that a woman somewhere in the world is
fated to bear a son "greater than his father;" if Zeus cannot discover her name
(which is known only to Prometheus), he must either give up his amatory pursuits
entirely or run the certain risk of being deposed in turn by his son. The woman
turns out to be the Nereid nymph Thetis; Zeus learns her identity and forces her to
marry the mortal Peleus (1006-1007). Another version suggests that the son who
will try to depose Zeus is the parthenogenic son of his final wife Hera, who will
bear an avenger because of her anger with Zeus. The *Theogony* mentions both the

by the advice of Gaia and starry Ouranos.° Thus
they advised him, so that no other of the eternal
gods would hold the office of king but Zeus.
For from her wise children were fated to be born:
first a daughter, owl-eyed Tritogeneia,°   895
like her father in strength and wise counsel,
but then she was going to bear a son
proud of heart, king of gods and men;
but first Zeus put her into his own belly,
so the goddess might advise him on good and evil.   900

· · · · · ·

Second, he married sleek Themis,° who bore the Horai,
Eunomia and Dike and blooming Eirene,

---

anger and the fatherless son, who is Hephaistos (927-928), but says nothing about a
conflict between Zeus and Hephaistos. In *Hh to Apollo* 305-356, Hera's anger also
leads to a parthenogenic birth, but the son is not Hephaistos but Typhoeus. Perhaps
the role of Typhoeus in the *Theogony* replaces that of Hephaistos in a lost myth,
traces of which may remain in the account of conflict between Zeus and Hephaistos
in *Iliad* 1. For these myths and their psychological significance see *Ps* 98-100. For
the "wisdom" demonstrated by Zeus see on 889-891 and *In* 16.

889-891 Since Metis, like all water-deities, can change her shape, Zeus seems to have
tricked her (with "wily words") into assuming a shape in which she could be easily
swallowed. Whatever the "wily words" may be, they seem to be the only instance
in this episode of Zeus taking the initiative in the use of "practical wisdom" [*metis*].
The actual swallowing seems due to the advice of Gaia and even more to the logic
of the succession myth, which would seem to leave Zeus no other alternative (*In*
16-17).

895 Athena's epithet "Tritogeneia" may mean "born by the river Triton," but this is by
no means certain.

901-906 Themis, Zeus' second wife, is of the Titan generation (135). As in the case of
Metis, her name indicates the benefit Zeus derives from alliance with her; themis
means "right" or "established custom." The children of Zeus and Themis are the
three Horai [Seasons]-Eunomia [Lawfulness], Dike [Justice], Eirene [Peace]-and
the three Moirai [Fates]-Klotho [Spinner], Lachesis [Allotter], Atropos [Unbend-
ing]. In cult the Horai are principally goddesses of the seasons and therefore of the
vegetative cycle (their Athenian cult names Thallo and Karpo mean "grow" and
"bear fruit"). The names given to them in the *Theogony* suggest that they function
in civic and political life as well, another area in which regularity and predictability
are essential. This is not an abrupt change; the connection between the farmer's
well-being and the need for good governance, as well as a marked emphasis on
Dike, are important in the *Works and Days*, especially in regard to Hesiod's personal problem with his brother Perses. The Moirai were earlier called daughters of
Night (217); the inconsistency may be due to the second poet's negligence (or Hesiod's), or to either poet's wish to present an alternate version. As their names suggest, they are the determiners of a lifetime, visualized as a thread which one spins,
the second measures, and the third fixes at the measured length, often by cutting it.

who tend the works of mortal men, and the
Moirai, to whom wise Zeus gave most honor,
Klotho and Lachesis and Atropos, who give   905
mortal men to have both good and evil.

Eurynome,° Okeanos' daughter of fairest form,
bore to him the three fair-cheeked Charites,
Aglaia, Euphrosyne, and lovely Thalia;
limb-loosening desire poured from their glancing   910
eyes; beautifully they glanced under their brows.

Next he came to the bed of nurturant Demeter;°
she bore white-armed Persephone, whom Aidoneus
seized from her mother; but Zeus allowed it.

Then he loved fair-haired Mnemosyne,° who bore   915
the nine Muses with golden headbands,
whose delight is banquets and the pleasure of song.

And Leto, joined in love to Zeus Aigiochos,°

They are birth spirits, occasionally appearing in myth to predict the destiny of a
new-born infant; the most famous instance is the birth of Meleagros (*Ap* 1.8.2). As
goddesses of destiny, they are involved with the value, as well as the length, of a
lifetime (906).

907-911 The third wife is the Okeanid Eurynome, whose three daughters are the
Charites-Aglaia [Splendor], Euphrosyne [Gladness], Thalia [Festivity]. Personifications of everything that is beautiful and graceful in nature and human life, they
seem also, like the Horai, to be associated with vegetative life; in Athenian cult one
of them is named Auxo [Increaser]. Charis (a singular form of Charites, like Moira
and Moirai) is the wife of Hephaistos at *Iliad* 18.362, while in the *Theogony* he is
married to Aglaia, youngest of the Charites (945-946). The description of the
Charites in 910-911 emphasizes their erotic attractiveness and desirability, and they
appear often as attendants of Aphrodite.

912-914 Zeus' fourth wife is his sister Demeter. The abduction of their daughter
Persephone by Hades, with the connivance of Zeus, is narrated most fully in the *Hh
to Demeter*. Both Demeter and her daughter are associated with vegetative phenomena, like the Horai and the Charites, and the two may originally have been two
aspects of the same goddess. Aidoneus is a lengthened form of the name Hades.
Apollodoros (1.3.1) calls Styx the mother of Persephone. See also on 454.

915-917 For Mnemosyne and the Muses, see on 53, 56-60, 75-79.

918-920 Leto is the daughter of the Titans Koios and Phoibe (404-406) and thus Zeus'
cousin. She appears frequently in lists of particularly important, prestigious, or sen-
ior goddesses (e.g., *Th* 18), probably because of her famous children. The difficult
birth of Apollo and Artemis is narrated first in the *Hh to Apollo*: Leto wandered
throughout the world in search of a place to bear her children, but every land was
afraid to be the birthplace of Apollo; finally the barren island of Delos consented,
after Leto promised that Apollo would have his temple there; Leto went into labor,
but Hera kept away her daughter Eileithyia, goddess of childbirth, and Leto's labor
was prolonged for nine days and nights; a committee of goddesses sent Iris to bribe
Eileithyia with a necklace and on Eileithyia's arrival Apollo was born (on the tenth

bore Apollo and archeress Artemis, beautiful
children beyond all of Ouranos' descendants.   920
   Lastly he made Hera his blooming wife;°
she bore Hebe and Ares and Eileithyia,
having joined in love with the king of gods and men.
   He himself bore from his head owl-eyed Athena,°
the awesome, fight-rousing, army-leading, unweary   925
mistress whose delight is din and wars and battles;
but Hera, who was angry and at odds with her husband,°
without love's union bore famous Hephaistos,
excellent in arts beyond all of Ouranos' descendants.
   From Amphitrite and loud-sounding Earth-Shaker°   930
was born great and mighty Triton,° who in the sea's

---

day of labor; for the ratio 9:1, see on 722-725). The Hymn says that Artemis was born on Ortygia and Apollo on Delos, but according to Apollodoros (1.4.1) both are names of the same island; Artemis was born first, then acted as midwife in the birth of her twin brother (this is apparently an attempt to justify the practice of invoking the virgin Artemis as a goddess who assists in births). See on 409.

921-923 The three children of Zeus and Hera, his seventh and permanent wife, are Hebe (goddess of youth), Ares (god of war), and Eileithyia (goddess of childbirth). None of them is particularly significant. Hebe, the personification of eternal pubescence, marries Herakles when he becomes a god (*Odyssey* 11.602-604). Ares appears in myth chiefly as the lover of Aphrodite (*Odyssey* 8.266-366), in the use of his name as a synonym for war, and occasionally as a participant (often unsuccessful) in battle (e.g., *Iliad* 5.835-863, 21.391-433). Eileithyia is primarily an agent of her mother's resentment against Zeus' mistresses, other wives, and illegitimate children; she interferes with the birth of Apollo and Artemis (see on 918-920) and with the birth of Herakles (*Ap* 2.4.5).

924-926 Since Athena has apparently been inside Zeus during six marriages, it is perhaps not surprising that artistic and literary representations of her birth portray her as a fully-grown, fully-armed adult (e.g., *Ap* 1.3.6). Either Hephaistos (Pindar, *Olympian* 7.65) or Prometheus (Euripides, *Ion* 454) splits open Zeus' head with an axe, so that Athena can be born.

927-929 Hera's quarrel with Zeus is the result of his having given birth to Athena; since he seems no longer to need a woman to produce a child, she decides to show him that she does not need a man to bear a child herself (*Hh to Apollo* 307-352; see *Ps* 99-102). Her first attempt results in the crippled Hephaistos, whom she throws out of the sky; her second produces the monster Typhoeus. Hephaistos, born from Hera's anger and desire for revenge, would seem to represent the fated son who will attempt to overthrow Zeus. Vestiges of this representation survive in *Iliad* 1.571-594, but this rebellious function is transferred almost entirely from Hephaistos to Prometheus and Typhoeus (*Ps* 98-102).

930 Finished with the children of Zeus and Hera, Hesiod moves to Zeus' brother Poseidon (Earth-Shaker); Hades and Persephone have no children, the only instance in Greek myth of a fruitless divine union. Amphitrite is a Nereid (243).

931-933 Triton is a Greek merman, half-man and half-fish, who is frequently depicted in decorative sculpture. His "awfulness" appears in stories like the one told by

depth lives with his mother and lord father in
olden homes, an awful god. But to Ares, piercer
of shields, Kythereia° bore Phobos and Deimos,
terrible ones who rout the dense ranks of men in   935
cold war with city-destroying Ares, and she bore
Harmonia, whom high-spirited Kadmos took as his wife.
  And the Atlantid Maia bore to Zeus glorious Hermes,°
herald of the gods, after going up to his holy bed.
  And the Kadmeid Semele° bore an illustrious son, much- 940
cheering Dionysos, after joining Zeus in love,
mortal with immortal; now they both are gods.
  And Alkmene bore mighty Herakles, having
joined in love with cloud-gathering Zeus.°
  And Hephaistos, the famous lame god, made Aglaia,° 945
youngest of the Charites, his blooming wife.

Pausanias (9.20) that Triton tried to rape the women of Boiotian Tanagra as they
bathed in the sea, but was prevented by Dionysos. The earliest surviving mention
of Triton is in the *Theoogony*, and it may be relevant that Hesiod, like the women
of Tanagra, is Boiotian.

934-937 Kythereia ["of the island Kythera"] is a title of Aphrodite (198). The sons of
Ares and Aphrodite are Phobos [Fear] and Deimos [Terror], personifications of
Ares' effect in battle. Kadmos is the founder of Boiotian Thebes; he kills a giant
serpent, Ares' son, and from the serpent's teeth grow the Spartoi [Sown-Men], the
first citizens of Thebes; he then is reconciled with Ares and marries his daughter
Harmonia (*Ap* 3.4.1-2).

938-939 According to Apollodoros (3.10.1-3, 3.12.1), Atlas and the Okeanid Pleione
had seven daughters called the Pleiades. Three of them have affairs with Zeus and
produce important sons: Taygete has Lakedaimon, Elektra has Dardanos (founder
of the Trojan dynasty), and Maia, the eldest, has Hermes. The story of Hermes'
birth and infancy, his invention of the lyre, and his quarrel with Apollo, is told in
the *Hh to Hermes*. Hermes is the herald, or messenger, of the gods because he is
the god of boundaries and of the crossing of boundaries; thus he passes between
mortals and immortals and also, as Hermes Psychopompos [the "Guide of Souls"],
between the living and the dead. A boundary marker in Athens was called simply a
hermes, a square pillar with a protruding phallus and Hermes' head.

940-942 Semele is the daughter of Kadmos and Harmonia (see on 933-937). For the
affair of Semele and Zeus, see *Ps* 94; from the ashes of the thunder-struck Semele,
Zeus rescued the foetus, put it in his thigh, and later gave birth to the god Dionysos
(Euripides, *Bacchai* 88-100). The deification of Semele seems to be due to the fact
that she was consumed by Zeus' lightning (Pindar, *Olympian* 2.25), rather than to
her role as mother of Dionysos.

943-944 See on 56-60.

945-946 See on 907-911.

And gold-haired Dionysos took auburn Ariadne,°
daughter of Minos, as his blooming wife;
Kronos' son made her immortal and ageless for him.
   The strong son of fair-ankled Alkmene, mighty   950
Herakles, having finished his painful labors, took
Hebe,° child of great Zeus and gold-sandaled Hera,
as his modest wife in snowy Olympos; he is
happy, who finished his great work and lives with
the immortals, carefree and ageless for all days.   955
   To untiring Helios the famed Okeanid Perseis°
bore Kirke and the king Aietes.
Aietes, son of Helios who shines on mortals,
by the gods' plans married fair-cheeked Idyia,
the daughter of the perfect river Okeanos;   960
she bore to him fine-ankled Medeia, conquered
in love thanks to golden Aphrodite.
   Farewell now, you who have Olympian homes,
you islands, mainland, and salty sea within;°
now, sweet-voiced Olympian Muses,° daughters of   965
Zeus Aigiochos, sing the band of goddesses,

947-949 Ariadne is the daughter of Minos, king of Crete. In the most common version,
she helps the Athenian prince Theseus escape from the labyrinth at Knossos and is
taken by him to the island of Naxos. There he abandons her, but Dionysos finds
and marries her. In Athens, on the second day (the "Choes" day) of the Anthesteria
festival, the marriage of Ariadne and Dionysos was re-enacted; Ariadne was played
by the wife of the archon basileus (the chief religious magistrate), and the god appeared either as a symbolic artifact or as a disguised man (or perhaps both).

950-955 For the marriage of Herakles and Hebe, see on 921-923. The "painful labors"
of Herakles are the tasks (usually twelve) he undertakes for Eurystheus, a punishment for having murdered his family while maddened by Hera (*Ap* 2.4.12-2.5.12);
see on 215-216, 289-294, 313-318, 327-332. The marriage of Herakles and Hebe,
which presupposes Herakles' deification, is one of the most frequently-cited reasons (along with the mention of Latinos and the Etruscans in 1013-1016) for re-
garding the ending of the *Theogony* as written by someone later than Hesiod, since
Herakles does not seem to be treated as a god before the sixth century (West, *T*
398, 417).

956-962 The children of Helios (371) and Perseis (356) are Kirke, the famous sorcer-
ess of the Odyssey, and Aietes, king of Kolchis and owner of the Golden Fleece at
the time of the Argonauts' voyage. The daughter of Aietes and the Okeanid Idyia
(352) is Medeia, who will marry Iason (1000) after helping him win the Fleece.

963-964 These two lines mark the end of the theogonic and cosmogonic purposes of
the poem; 963 bids farewell to stories of gods (as opposed to goddesses) and their
children, and 964 to the physical components of the visible world.

965-968 The subject of the remainder of the *Theogony* is stated; it is a new subject and
so the Muses are invoked anew.

immortals who went to bed with mortal men
and bore children similar to gods.

The divine goddess Demeter,° joined in dear love
with the hero Iasion in a thrice-plowed field,   970
in the rich land of Crete, bore kindly Ploutos,
who goes over the whole earth and the sea's wide
backs; who meets him and takes him in his arms,
the god makes rich and grants him much prosperity.

Harmonia, daughter of golden Aphrodite, to Kadmos°   975
bore Ino and Semele and fair-cheeked Agaue
and Autonoe, whom long-haired Aristaios married,
and Polydoros in well-crowned Thebes.

Kallirhoe,° Okeanos' daughter, joined in golden
Aphrodite's love to strong-hearted Chrysaor,   980
bore a son, the strongest of all mortals,
Geryoneus, whom mighty Herakles killed in
sea-swept Erytheia for his rolling-gaited cattle.°

And Eos bore to Tithonos bronze-crested Memnon,°
king of the Aithiopes, and the lord Emathion.   985
And to Kephalos she bore a glorious son, valiant

969-974 The union of Demeter and Iasion in a thrice-plowed field is mentioned by
Homer (*Odyssey* 5.125-128) and must reflect a ritual practice intended to promote
the fertility of the fields; this is why their son is Ploutos [Wealth]. The hero Iasion
seems here to be Cretan, although we never hear of Cretan parents for him; Apollodoros makes him a son of Zeus and Elektra (3.12.1; see on 938-939). Both Homer
and Apollodoros say that Iasion paid for his erotic ambition by being struck with
Zeus' lightning.

975-978 The children of Harmonia and Kadmos: the unfortunate Ino, wife of the
Boiotian king Athamas, tried to kill her step-children and then killed her own son
and herself (*Ap* 1.9.1-2); transformed into the sea-goddess Leukothea, she gives an
immortal veil to Odysseus in *Odyssey* 5.333-353. For Semele see on 940-942.
Agaue is the mother of the Theban king Pentheus; in Euripides' *Bacchai* Pentheus
is seduced by his enemy Dionysos into spying on the god's secret rites, whereupon
the ecstatic Agaue mistakes her son for a lion and tears off his head. Aristaios, a
son of Apollo, and Autonoe are the parents of Aktaion, who chances to see the goddess Artemis naked and is punished by being torn to pieces by his own hunting
dogs (*Ap* 3.4.4). Polydoros is the father of Labdakos and great-grandfather of
Oidipous (Euripides, *Phoinissai* 7-9).

979-983 The son of Kallirhoe (288, 351) and Chrysaor (281) is the triple-bodied (or -
headed) Geryoneus (287).

982-983 is a restatement of 289-290.

984-991 The rapacious goddess Eos [Dawn], although married to Astraios (378), is
continually carrying off other men; Apollodoros (1.4.4) says that her affair with
Ares angered Aphrodite, who caused Eos to be continually in love. By the Trojan

Phaethon, a man like the gods; when he was young
in the delicate flower of famous youth, a child
of tender thoughts, laughter-loving Aphrodite
snatched him up and took and made him innermost   990
keeper of her holy temples, a godlike daimon.°
    Aison's son,° by the plans of the eternal gods,
took from Aietes, god-raised king, his daughter,
having finished the many painful labors
which the great and arrogant king assigned,   995
Pelias, violent and impetuous doer of wrong;
having finished these, Aison's son came to Iolkos°
after much labor, bringing the glancing girl
on the swift ship, and made her his fresh bride.
Tamed by Iason, shepherd of the people, she   1000
bore a son Medeios, whom Phillyra's son Cheiron
raised in the mountains; great Zeus' will was done.

Tithonos she bore Memnon, king of Troy's allies, the Aithiopes, and Emathion.
Zeus granted her request that Tithonos be immortal, but she forgot to ask also that
he be ageless; finally he was reduced to a babbling and shriveled wreck (*Hh to
Aphrodite* 218-238). Memnon is killed in the Trojan War by Achilleus, and
Emathion is killed by Herakles during his eleventh labor (*Ap* E.5.3, 2.5.11). The
Athenian Kephalos, son of Hermes, Deion, or Pandion, is married to Prokris,
daughter of the Athenian king Erechtheus; carried off by Eos, he becomes the fa-
ther of Phaethon, whom Aphrodite abducts in emulation of Zeus' rape of
Ganymedes. In Euripides' lost Phaethon, Phaethon is a son of Helios who takes his
father's chariot and horses on an ill-fated joy-ride.

992-996 Aison's son is Iason, leader of the Argonauts; the daughter of Aietes is
Medeia (957-962); the "many painful labors" which Aietes compels Iason to per-
form before he can receive the Golden Fleece are, at least in later versions, accomplished for the most part by Medeia on her helpless lover's behalf. Pelias is a "doer
of wrong" because, among other crimes, he seized the kingdom of Iolkos from
Aison, Iason's father and the rightful king.

997-1002 Upon arriving in Iolkos, Medeia tricks the daughters of Pelias into killing
their father, thus winning revenge for Iason just as she had won for him the Golden
Fleece. Medeios, the son of Iason and Medeia, is the namesake of the Medes. Usually (as in Euripides' *Medea*) the sons of Iason and Medeia are killed by their
mother to punish Iason, who has left her for another woman, and Medeios (or Me-
dos) is the son of Medeia and Aigeus, a king of Athens (*Ap* 1.9.28). Medeios is one
of several heroes raised and educated by the wise centaur Cheiron in his famous
cave on Mount Pelion overlooking the bay of Iolkos (modern Volos). Phillyra is a
daughter of Okeanos, according to a fragment from the lost epic Gigantomachy
(the War with the Giants); Cheiron's father is Kronos, and the fact that Cheiron is
half-horse, half-man is due to the fact that Kronos assumed the shape of a stallion
to have sex with Phillyra (supposedly to escape the notice of his wife Rhea, or because Phillyra first changed herself into a mare).

As for the daughters of Nereus,° old man of the sea,
the divine goddess Psamathe bore Phokos from the
love of Aiakos, thanks to golden Aphrodite;   1005
and the silver-shod goddess Thetis, tamed by Peleus,
bore Achilleus, the lion-spirited manslayer.°
 And well-crowned Kythereia bore Aineias, having
joined in dear love with the hero Anchises
on the peaks of windy Ida with many glens.°   1010
 And Kirke,° daughter of the Hyperionid Helios,
in the love of patient-minded Odysseus bore
Agrios and Latinos, blameless and strong;
[and she bore Telegonos thanks to golden Aphrodite]
far away in a niche of holy islands   1015
they ruled over all the famous Tyrsenians.
 The divine goddess Kalypso,° joined to Odysseus
in dear love, bore Nausithoos and Nausinoos.

1003-1005 The Nereid Psamathe (260) has an affair with Aiakos, king of the island Aigina and husband of Endeis. Their son Phokos (see on 260) is killed by his better-known half-brothers Telamon (an ally and lover of Herakles) and Peleus, the future father of Achilleus (*Ap* 3.12.6, 2.6.4).

1006-1007 See *Ps* 97-98.

1008-1010 The affair of Aphrodite and the Trojan shepherd Anchises is told in the *Hh to Aphrodite*. Zeus, blaming Aphrodite for the compulsion felt by himself and other gods to have sexual relations with mortals, inflicts a similar passion on the goddess; disguising herself as a mortal woman, she appears to Anchises, who falls in love and takes her to bed; afterwards the goddess reveals herself, announces that she will bear him a son Aineias, and warns that Zeus will strike Anchises with lightning if he reveals her name. Ida is a mountain of Troy, not the famous Mount Ida of Crete (see on 481-484). Aineias is the famous hero of the foundation of Rome in the Roman poet Vergil's epic *Aeneid*.

1011-1016 Kirke (957), the enchantress who turns Odysseus' men into animals in *Odyssey* 10, is usually the mother (and Odysseus the father) of Telegonos; the weight of this tradition is probably the reason why 1014 was inserted at some unknown time. Agrios may be associated with Faunus, who is the father of Latinus in one branch of early Italian myth (West, *T* 434). Latinus is the legendary king of the Latins, whom Aineias meets upon arriving in Italy, and the Tyrsenians are the Etruscans, the earliest historical inhabitants of Italy north of Rome. Although the author of 1015 seems to have little idea of the whereabouts of these peoples (somewhere in a "niche of holy islands"), knowledge of Latins and Tyrsenians (Etruscans), living somewhere to the west, must have been available in Greece during the second half of the 6th century (West, *T* 436).

1017-1018 Atlas' daughter Kalypso (see on 359) is the nymph who keeps Odysseus in amiable servitude for seven years (*Odyssey* 7.244-263). She is childless in the *Odyssey*; of the two sons here given to her, Nausithoos is the name of the first king of the Phaiakians in the *Odyssey* (7.56-62). Since Odysseus comes directly from Ka-

These are the immortals who went to bed with°
mortal men and bore children similar to gods.°   1020
Now, sweet-voiced Olympian Muses, daughters of
Zeus Aigiochos, sing of the race of women]°

lypso to the Phaiakians, where Nausithoos' son Alkinoos currently rules, the
Phaiakian Nausithoos can hardly be the son of Odysseus and Kalypso; Homer, in
fact, calls Nausithoos the son of Poseidon and Periboia. Nausinoos, which sounds
also like a Phaiakian name (cf. Nausikaa), is otherwise unknown.

1019-1020 These two lines are virtually identical with 967-968, and mark the conclusion of the type of genealogies promised in the earlier passage.

1021-1022 These two lines repeat 965-966 with only one word changed-"women" for
"goddesses." A new subject is being introduced, with the Muses' help, and it must
be the *Catalogue of Women* (see on 886-929).

Interpretation:

The Psychology of the Succession Myth

This interpretation of the *Theogony* depends on two basic assumptions. The first is that all human beings have, and use, a mode of thinking which is inaccessible to ordinary consciousness. This hidden world of thought is nothing mystical; it is the ideas and fantasies, typically originating in the childhood experiences which form our personalities and often connected in some way with our adult life, which are kept in a state of permanent repression (that is, kept out of consciousness by an internal censoring process).

The second assumption is that myths, like dreams, express these unconscious ideas in a more or less disguised, or symbolic, form. Dreams seem to have two positive functions: to protect sleep by incorporating potential disturbances (such as hunger, noise, etc.) into a dream, and to protect mental stability by relaxing repression temporarily and allowing repressed ideas to enter dream-consciousness in some form. Recent studies of the physiology of dreaming, at any rate, have shown that people who are deprived of dreams (but not of sleep) within a few days begin to hallucinate, become depressed and anxious, and exhibit quasi-psychotic personality traits.

Myths, of course, have many functions: they can entertain, they can instruct, they can remember, they can justify, and so on. But there are two functions, related to one another, which seem to be operative in nearly all myths: to satisfy curiosity, and (like dreams) to express unconscious fantasies.

It might be objected at this point that the satisfaction of curiosity could hardly be a primary motive of myths, since it is essential that myths be repeated over and over, whereas curiosity would presumably be exhausted after the first telling. To answer this objection, we need only recall the universal demand of small children that their favorite stories be told again and again, their insistence that they be repeated faithfully and accurately (and also the mixture of joy and exasperation with which they greet any deviation). It may be that a compulsion to repeat is present here; that is, the pleasure of curiosity's initial satisfaction is so great that the experience can be repeated many times. But it is probably better to assume that the satisfaction (and re-satisfaction) of curiosity is combined with another function related to the child's emotional needs. In other words, there are two simultaneous satisfactions, one intellectual and the other emotional, which work together; the first achieves its purpose by answering questions, and the second in a number of ways (mastering fear, resolving emotional ambivalence, identification with a relevant character, etc.). When the evil stepmother disappears and the fairy godmother returns in the nick of time, the child learns two things: on an intellectual level, he learns how the story ends; on an emotional level, he realizes that the bad mother (who is in reality the punishing, disappointing, denying, or merely absent mother) is only a temporary presence, and that the real mother is the good mother who will surely return.

Myths also satisfy curiosity of many different kinds, although the underlying question is always "What was it like in the past?" In the case of a theogony, the object of curiosity is how the world began, how things started, how the world and its gods came to be the way it is believed they are. But this intellectual function is inseparable from an emotional goal, just as the child's question "Where do babies come from?" is really an expression of his concern over the details of his own conception, birth, and status.

The symbolic expression of unconscious needs energizes the other functions of myth. It is what makes myths moving and compelling, even for someone who no longer believes in their literal truth, and (just as in dreams) it attaches emotional energy to a varied, often seemingly unconnected, collection of memories. The most important difference, although not the only one, between myths and dreams is that dreams express the wishes and fears of a single individual, and these may be so personal and idiosyncratic, so tied up in an individual history, that they may be irrelevant or nonexistent for others. Myths, however, whatever their hypothetical beginning may have been, retain their status as myth only if the wishes and fears they express pertain to many or all of a population.

We should begin our study of the *Theogony* by returning to the issue of curiosity. To be curious about all sorts of matters is natural and appropriate for children; it is how they learn and grow, and its gradual loss is one of the unfortunate disasters of maturation. Among all the objects of childhood curiosity, however, there are two matters of special importance for dreams and myths, because they are intimately connected with the child's feelings and are most likely to produce anxiety and subsequent repression: the origin of the baby, and the difference between the sexes.

It is not difficult to see that these questions are really about the child's own birth and status, and about parental sexuality. The question "Where do babies come from?" is really a generalized expression of two questions of great emotional significance to the child: "Where did I come from?" and "How did my parents produce me?".

We might expect to find symbolic representations of these questions and their answers, and of the fantasies and memories associated with them, occurring frequently in myth. Every birth of a hero, for example, reflects to some extent the individual's repressed curiosity and ideas about the circumstances of his own birth. But it is especially in myths of the beginning of the world that we might anticipate finding a mythical version of the beginning of the individual.

The world, according to Hesiod, begins with the spontaneous emergence of four uncaused entities (116-120): Chaos, Gaia, Tartaros, and Eros. Why these four, and why in this order? Chaos signifies in Greek a void or abyss, a vast and impenetrable darkness (see on 116). This totally undifferentiated state is followed by the appearance of Gaia, the earth and, from both an anthropomorphic and a psychological viewpoint, the cosmic projection of the mother (see on 117).

If we regard the account of the world's beginning as a mythical representation of unconscious memories pertaining to the beginning of individual life, we may suppose that Chaos must symbolize a stage of life before any perception of the mother exists. There is in fact such a stage, which lasts for approximately the first six months of a child's life, and it is generally referred to in psychoanalytic language as the "symbiotic" state. The leading characteristic of this state is the child's inability to perceive the difference between itself and its environment; I and not-I, child and mother, self and world, are not differentiated from one another in a clear or stable way.

Around the middle of the first year of post-natal existence, this state comes to an end and the child becomes an individual, able to discern the difference between self and others; the new stage is called "separation-individuation." Although this transition is a gradual process rather than a sudden event, the key factor on which self-recognition depends seems to be a prior perception of the mother (or whoever functions as the mother) as separate. Only when the child realizes that the mother is a separate person (whose return, whenever she leaves the child, is thus always a question and a source of anxiety) is he able to view himself, as if in a mirror, as a separate individual.

The beginning of individuation is therefore the occasion for emergence of a self-identity, a rudimentary "ego"; but it is also the time when anxiety, frustration, and desire are experienced for the first time. During symbiosis pain and discomfort, as well as pleasure and gratification, are felt by the child, but they are not experienced as dependent upon something or someone external to the child. The newborn infant does not cry because he is left alone, nor does he even know that he is alone. The individuated child, however, perceives that most of his needs and wishes (which are few but urgent) depend for their fulfillment on a separate entity, the mother. It is only when the child is able to recognize that something is absent or lacking that frustration can occur, and the desire to have something depends on the prior recognition of not having it.

Although the symbiotic state is left forever, unconscious memories remain of a situation in which there can be no desire, since nothing is perceived as missing or separate from the all-inclusive symbiotic "self." These memories appear most obviously, in the myths of Greece and of virtually all cultures, as stories of a primal paradise at the beginning of the human race, a situation in which the first humans lead a life of total comfort and ease without pain, labor, or desire. The Garden of Eden in *Genesis* is the most familiar example of this paradisal fantasy, but there are parallels everywhere, including several in Greek myth; the closest is Hesiod's myth of the Golden Race, in which the first men are portrayed as living in happiness and abundance, "free of troubles and misery" and effortlessly possessing "all good things" (*WD* 109-120).

The symbiotic Golden Race appears only in the *Works and Days*, however, while the *Theogony* portrays symbiosis under another aspect: as an undifferentiated state prior to the emergence of the mother as the first object of the child's perception. The mythical name of this formless state is Chaos and the end of this state, in myth as in life, is brought about by the fact that what was once part of the self is now a separate object, the mother or Gaia.

At this point in the mythical drama, symbiosis has ended and individuation has begun. The new individual experiences for the first time frustration and, as a result, desire for what is not present—for the mother, for gratification, and ultimately (and unconsciously) for restoration of the lost symbiotic state. This experience of primal lack and the beginning of desire, based on the perception of the mother as separate, occurs in Hesiod's myth as the appearance of Tartaros and Eros immediately after Gaia.

In the *Theogony* Tartaros is both the underworld in general and the lowest place in the underworld (720-721), and it is a place of punishment. The Titans and the monster Typhoeus are put there after their defeat by Zeus (729-730, 868), and it seems to be the place where Ouranos confines his children (see on 119, 154-160). In subsequent Greek literature, Tartaros was gradually identified as that part of the underworld in which certain famous sinners suffered specific punishments. Although the list eventually became rather full, the four earliest and best-known sufferers in Tartaros are Tityos, Sisyphos, Tantalos, and Ixion. Their punishments all signify frustration, not only in the general sense of being confined and restrained but also in the specific details of each case. Tityos is tied down while two vultures eat his liver, which grows back monthly only to be eaten again; Sisyphos rolls a huge stone uphill, whereupon it rolls back down on him; Tantalos is perpetually hungry and thirsty, standing amid fruit and water which always elude his grasp; Ixion is fastened to a fiery wheel which perpetually revolves.

The crimes of these four, like their punishments, are also variations on the same theme. Tityos and Ixion both tried to rape one of Zeus' wives (Leto in the case of the former and Hera in the latter). Sisyphos saw Zeus' rape of Aigina and told her father Asopos. Tantalos' crime appears in three variants: he revealed the gods' secrets, or he stole ambrosia, or he killed his son Pelops, cooked him, and fed him to the gods. We will return shortly to the psychological meaning of these crimes.

Tartaros is therefore a place not only of punishment, but also of eternal frustration and loss. In the *Theogony* as well as in later accounts it is where the losers in generational conflict and unsuccessful usurpers are confined. But in its first appearance, immediately after Gaia, Tartaros is a cosmic principle which represents the first crucial loss in the life of every individual—the irreversible loss of the symbiotic state and of the mother who has come to represent the earlier state of bliss.

This loss is the cause and condition of the first emergence of desire, which appears in the Hesiodic myth as Eros, fourth and last of the spontaneous primal beings. Hesiod's Eros is virtually an abstraction, a procreative principle in life and the cosmos; after Eros comes into existence, desire will be the controlling force in the development of the universe. But the immediate cause of the appearance of Eros is the prior existence of Tartaros. Frustration, the perception that something is lacking, is the necessary antecedent of desire, as Socrates says in the *Symposium* (200e): "Eros is always the desire of something, and that something is what is lacking." Or, in Hesiod's mythic terminology, Tartaros must come before Eros.

The first great loss for every individual is the loss of symbiosis, and the first desire is the impossible wish to recover that state. The cycle of lack and desire will continue in innumerable forms throughout life, once the individual has recognized that the absent objects which will fulfill desire are located outside himself and his control. But the next time that we find the combination of impossible desire and inevitable loss occurs at the time of the oedipus complex, the climactic episode of childhood psychological development. The oedipus complex may be defined most generally as the child's possessive and jealous wishes concerning the parent of the opposite sex and related feelings of rivalry and hostility toward the parent of the same sex. In the case of the male child (the usual reference in Greek myth), this involves the son's desire to replace his father in the attention and affection of his mother, and his fantasies both of removing the father and of gratifying the mother in whatever way she requires (and in whatever way the child imagines that the father performs this task).

The oedipus complex is of course the basic principle of the *Theogony*'s narrative plot, a cycle of generational conflict in which mothers favor their sons and sons overcome their fathers, until Zeus finally puts an end to the repetitive pattern. But the oedipus complex is also a critical re-statement of the inevitable loss and impossible desire which characterize the end of symbiosis in particular and the situation of individuated life in general.

This reciprocity appears in Hesiod's portrayal of Tartaros as both a primal being and as a prison for oedipal criminals. The situation of the Titans is somewhat different from that of the four criminals later placed in Tartaros, since the Titans are at least partially successful in their oedipal endeavor. Ouranos also had succeeded in part, marrying his mother but not overthrowing his father (he doesn't have one), and the Titans overthrow their father but do not marry their mother. It is, in fact, only after the appearance of Zeus that the impossibility of oedipal desire is established. He cannot be overthrown, and since removal of the father is a prerequisite to possession of the mother, the oedipal project is henceforth doomed to failure.

The two key instances in the *Theogony* of an unsuccessful oedipal rebellion against Zeus are his conflicts with the monster Typhoeus and the Titan Prometheus. Neither of these potential usurpers is actually a son of Zeus, but, as we shall see, both of them are substitutes for an identifiable son. In particular, the struggle between Zeus and Prometheus in the central panel of the *Theogony* is clearly related to the situation of the oedipal criminals in Tartaros; his punishment is almost exactly the same as that of Tityos, and his crimes are similar to those of Tantalos. Prometheus steals the gods' fire and Tantalos steals their ambrosia, and both of them attempt to deceive the gods at a banquet.

At this point it may be helpful to look more closely at the crimes of the four inhabitants of Tartaros. If we assume that the gods are psychological representations of the parents, and in particular that Zeus represents the father, the meaning and similarity of these crimes is apparent. Ixion and Tityos are the most straightforwardly oedipal, since each of them attempts to rape one of Zeus' wives. The crime of Sisyphos, that he spied on Zeus' sexual activity and then revealed the "secret," is also oedipal, a fulfillment of the child's wish to see a forbidden sexual sight and to learn the secrets of parental sexuality.

Tantalos, like Sisyphos, is said to have revealed the "secrets" of the gods (*Ap* E.2.1), and the oedipal nature of this crime appears also in his other two crimes: 1) he stole ambrosia, and 2) he was so obsessed with proving himself superior to the gods that he cut up and served his son Pelops to the gods for dinner, figuring that if any of the gods ate a piece of Pelops, this would prove that he knew something they did not know (Pindar, *Olympian* 1). The cannibalistic banquet is both oedipal and "counter-oedipal": at the same time that he attempts to prove himself superior to Zeus (who is his real, as well as symbolic, father), Tantalos tries to eliminate the potential threat of his own son (just as Ouranos and Kronos tried to do).

Tantalos' theft of ambrosia, like the theft of fire by Prometheus, is the metaphoric expression of an oedipal desire not only because each substance is a jealously guarded divine (i.e., paternal) prerogative, but also because both ambrosia and fire have demonstrable sexual meanings. Ambrosia is relatively unimportant in Greek myth, but its symbolic meaning can be seen by comparing it to its linguistic and mythical equivalent in Hindu myth, the divine food called *amrta* in Sanskrit. Both *ambrosia* and *amrta* literally mean "immortality," and that is what consumption of these foods confers on the Greek and Hindu gods. But, in addition, *amrta* and *soma* (the other and more common Sanskrit word for ambrosia) are explicitly associated in Hindu myth with semen and paternal sexuality. There are numerous Hindu myths of the theft of amrta or soma from the gods, which are similar to (and often combined with) stories of the theft of fire (which also symbolizes paternal sexuality). Greek and Hindu myths are both Indo-European, and there would seem to be a vast and pervasive Indo-European complex of myths in which the theft of fire or the food of immortality represents an oedipal assault on the paternal privileges of the sky-god.

Even if we did not know about the Hindu parallels and other Indo-European material, however, there is ample evidence in Greek myth that the thefts of fire and ambrosia are symbolic equivalents, and that both represent an attempt to take for oneself the sexual position of the father-god. Although Prometheus is not punished in Tartaros as is Tantalos, the nature of the punishment he receives is almost exactly the same as that of Tityos, who is in Tartaros; both are confined while a bird or birds eat their livers, which are periodically renewed after being consumed. If the punishments of Prometheus and Tityos are the same, their crimes are presumably equivalent, and Tityos' attempted rape of Zeus' wife is an oedipal offense.

The same principle holds true for Tantalos, who is in Tartaros for stealing ambrosia. Since the crimes of the others who are there, as well as his own crimes in other versions, are overtly oedipal, the theft of ambrosia would also seem to be oedipal. Furthermore, ambrosia (in Tantalos' crime) and fire (in Prometheus' crime) are structurally equivalent, as we have seen, and fire (especially the fiery lightning-bolt) is associated with the sky-god's sexual power in Greek and other myths.

The first of the Greek sky-gods is Ouranos, whose marriage to his mother Gaia establishes an oedipal precedent from the beginning. This union of Ouranos and Gaia, Sky and Earth, creates an interesting problem: if they are to be the first parents, how do they join together to produce children? How can the sexual intercourse of Sky and Earth be represented? The obvious, and perhaps earliest, answer is that the rain which falls from the sky onto the earth is the semen of Ouranos. As Aeschylus says in a fragment of his tragedy *Danaides*, "Rain falling from Ouranos makes Gaia pregnant." The same symbolism underlies the frequent occurrence in many origin myths of water and earth as the elements from which a creator-god makes the first humans, as in Hesiod's account of the creation of Pandora by Hephaistos (*WD* 60-61). In some instances this creative clay is made from earth and spit, and the sexual symbolism is more explicit; the water which impregnates earth is a bodily fluid (the same symbolism appears in the English saying that someone is the "spit and image of his father"). The most obvious sexual allusion, however, appears in the word ouranos itself, a noun related to the verb ourein ("to urinate"). Ouranos, he-who-rains, is in fact "he-who-urinates."

The other means by which the sky comes into contact with the earth, and therefore the other cosmic symbol for the sky-god's sexual power, is lightning. This significance not only appears in references by Greek philosophers to fire as the generative element in nature, but also plays a role in the myth of Zeus' affair with Semele, a mortal princess of Thebes. Tricked by Hera into insisting that Zeus have sex with her in the same way that he did with his divine wife, Semele was incinerated by the lightning of Zeus, who burst through the bedroom door driving a chariot and hurling thunderbolts. The sexual power of Zeus is a force so powerful that no mortal woman can tolerate its full expression, and its symbol is the fire of Zeus' lightning.

The elemental opposites fire and water, lightning and rain, are thus the cosmic projections of the sky-god's paternal sexuality, and the theft of fire by Prometheus is an oedipal attack on Zeus. The first oedipal revolt in the *Theogony*, however, occurs in the first generation of the gods. Ouranos, married to his own mother, tries to prevent his sons from overthrowing him and taking away his privileges. Gaia and her sons then conspire together to defeat Ouranos, who is castrated by Kronos, the younger generation becomes the older, and the sons become the new fathers. But if this is true, why do the Titans not try to marry their mother Gaia, just as Ouranos had married his? Although the ultimate goal of the oedipus complex is presumably the fulfillment of the son's wish to become the sexual partner of his mother, there is no indication that the Titans want or attempt to marry their mother. Four of the Titans sons marry their sisters (Okeanos marries

Tethys, Hyperion Theia, Koios Phoibe, and Kronos Rhea), Kreios marries his half-sister Eurybia, and Iapetos marries his niece Klymene. Gaia does in fact marry another of her sons after the downfall of Ouranos, but her new husband is not one of the Titans; he is her youngest parthenogenic son Pontos, by whom she gives birth to three sons and two daughters (233-239).

An answer to this problem, which will be repeated in the case of Zeus, is that the succession myth presents a kind of progression in which each generation tries to get what it wants without repeating the mistakes of the previous generation. Thus the Titans deposed their father and won his sexual power but then, not wanting to suffer the same fate as he had incurred, they chose to exercise their new sexual freedom by marrying their sisters or other relatives but not their mother.

Nevertheless, the sexual nature of the conflict between the Titans and their father is made clear by its outcome in the fact of castration. Furthermore, Gaia is not entirely absent from the sexual objective of her son Kronos, who replaces his father as lord of the sky and marries Rhea, his sister but also an earth-goddess like her mother Gaia. The same thing will happen in the next generation when Zeus, the third sky-god, marries the earth-goddesses Themis and Demeter.

As we have seen (*In* 17), the steps Kronos takes to protect his position are clearly derived from his memory of what had happened to his father and from his intention that nothing similar happen to himself. The lesson Kronos learns from the fate of Ouranos is basically misogynistic; he sees that it is the woman as much as the son who is his enemy. His children must not be allowed an independent existence, and they must be kept away from their mother, their potential accomplice. For these reasons Kronos decides to swallow each of his children as they are born, but his strategy fails and once again the sky-god is overthrown by his deceiving wife and ambitious son.

The filial agent of Kronos' defeat is his youngest son Zeus, and the fact that he is youngest is appropriate to his role as the successor of Kronos, just as Kronos was the youngest of the children of Ouranos. In myth it is typically the youngest son who inherits the father's position, and it is not difficult to see the psychological reason for this in the dynamics of sibling relationships. From the perspective of an older child, it is always the youngest who inherits, who displaces his predecessors in the affection and attention of his parents. In the Greek succession myth the conflict between the societal law of primogeniture (inheritance by the eldest) and the psychological law that the youngest child must usurp the privileged position of his older brothers is neatly solved by the imprisonment of the children as they are born in one or another parental body. When the Titans are released from the body of Gaia or when the Olympians are disgorged from the body of Kronos (in each case, a kind of second birth), the order of birth is reversed. Kronos, the youngest of the Titans, is closest to the surface of Earth and thus the first to be (re)born, and Zeus, youngest of the children of Kronos, moves to the position of eldest by escaping being swallowed and subsequent rebirth. In this way youngest becomes eldest, and psychological reality is mythically verified.

The conflict between Ouranos and Kronos had ended in an actual castration, such a conclusion being not only psychologically appropriate but also literally necessary in order for the children to escape from their mother's body. Now, in the second generation, freedom and victory are not simultaneous, as in the first, but are separate events; the children are freed by the ruse of the same Gaia who gave Kronos the sickle, and victory is later achieved by the superior power of Zeus and his allies. Although Kronos does not suffer a literal castration, he and his defeated fellow-Titans are imprisoned in Tartaros, a place of symbolic castration, and it should also be noted that the weapon which gives Zeus his military superiority is the lightning which represents his sexual preeminence.

Now that Zeus has become the new sky-god and lord of the universe, he faces two related tasks: he must find a way of avoiding the fate suffered by his father and grandfather, and he must then populate the world with the gods and heroes whose production will consume most of his time and energy from now on. The second task, which will establish the structure of Greek heroic myth, depends on completion of the first, since it is the security Zeus wins which gives him the opportunity of virtually unchecked procreation. The first task is also both climax and conclusion of the succession myth; by succeeding in it, Zeus will escape from the cycle of oedipal overthrow which conquered his predecessors.

The logically necessary solution discovered by Zeus (*In* 17-18) is to swallow his first wife Metis. Kronos had erred in thinking that he could succeed by separating his sons from their mother, but Zeus now realizes that the real enemy is his wife, and by swallowing Metis he prevents the birth of the son who is destined to overthrow him. This is only the first step in Zeus' strategy, however; he has a dual problem, wife and sons, and he will deal with each part of the problem separately. The seven wives of Zeus are, in order, the Okeanid nymph Metis, the Titanid Themis, another Okeanid Eurynome, Zeus' sister Demeter, another Titanid Mnemosyne, the second-generation Titanid Leto, and finally his sister Hera; the relationships of the seven to Zeus are cousin-aunt-cousin-sister-aunt-cousin-sister. Once he has secured his reign by swallowing Metis, the first wife, it seems that all other possible relationships are now open to him.

There is, of course, one important exception: unlike Ouranos, who had married his mother Gaia, and like Kronos and the Titans, who married their sisters but not their mother, Zeus stops short of mating with his mother Rhea. Nevertheless, just as Rhea had been virtually a mother-figure to her husband Kronos, Zeus now marries two of his mother's sisters (Themis and Mnemosyne) and two earth-goddesses (Themis and Demeter). But since marrying mother-substitutes instead of the actual mother had not saved Kronos from being overthrown, Zeus must do more than merely refrain from marrying Rhea herself.

Or, to put it another way, Kronos may be said to have married his mother under the guise of Rhea, her double, just as Ouranos had married his mother Gaia. With Zeus it seems that the scenario will be repeated again, since both maternal figures, Gaia and Rhea, contrive to save him from his father. But in Zeus' case there is an important difference: although he has a sexual relationship with two aunts and several maternal goddesses, he observes at least a rudimentary distinction between permissible and non-permissible sexual objects. His establishment of a primal incest taboo occurs in his first marriage; to avoid having the son who will overthrow him, Zeus must give up the woman who will be that son's mother.

Zeus then proceeds to atone for this act of restraint by copulating with practically every woman in Greek myth. There is, however, one other occasion on which he is forced to limit his sexual activity, a limitation perhaps required by the fact that he had not abstained entirely from a sexual relationship with Metis. In a myth appearing in several variants, Zeus is said to have learned that an unnamed woman was fated to bear a son who would be greater than his father. There could be no worse news for Zeus than this, since, if that woman exists somewhere in the world, she may be the next conquest in his procreation campaign. If he cannot discover her name, he must abandon sex or be overthrown. The one person who knows the identity of this woman is Prometheus, who has been sentenced by Zeus to eternal torture for his theft of fire, and he is not about to do an unrequited favor for Zeus. Once again Zeus has a simple choice and an inescapable decision: he must either give up sex entirely (which he cannot do), or he must free Prometheus in return for the name of the one woman he must renounce. He of course chooses the latter, and discovers that the woman is the Nereid nymph Thetis—who is, in one version, the current object of Zeus' amatory attention (*Ap* 3.13.5). Zeus forces Thetis to marry the mortal Peleus, a hero but not too much of one (having been defeated in wrestling by a woman, Atalante), and their son is Achilleus (1006-1007), a truly great hero but not the new sky-god.

Just as there are two occasions on which Zeus' strategy of observing at least a minimal restraint in regard to a current or potential wife is successful, the *Theogony* contains two exemplary instances in which he succeeds in overcoming an attempted oedipal rebellion. The success of his first strategy clearly does not imply that his position is free from attack, but rather that any oedipal assault on him will fail. Each of these two examples of unsuccessful rebellion occupies a prominent position in the *Theogony*; the first is the conflict of Zeus with Prometheus (521-616) and the second is his war with Typhoeus (820-868). The most obvious fact about both of Zeus' rivals is that neither of them is his son. Nevertheless both of them are closely connected with a god who may or may not be the son of Zeus and Hera, and who may be the oedipal rival underlying the myths of Prometheus and Typhoeus. This god is Hephaistos, the "Lame One," the god of metallurgy, fire, and magic.

In the *Odyssey* Hephaistos is the son of Zeus and Hera (8.312); in the *Iliad* the same parentage is assumed by most readers of 1.578 and 14.338, although the identification is somewhat ambiguous. In Hesiod's account (927-929), however, and in most post-Hesiodic versions he is the parthenogenic son of Hera alone. According to Hesiod, Hera produced the fatherless Hephaistos because she was angry with Zeus. Although the cause of her wrath is not mentioned by Hesiod, the preceding three verses (which interrupt the account of Zeus' marriage with Hera) tell how Zeus "himself bore from his head owl-eyed Athena," the daughter with whom Metis had been pregnant when Zeus swallowed her. It appears that the cause of the quarrel was Zeus' newfound ability to produce children by himself, a slight to which Hera responded with the parthenogenesis of Hephaistos.

The defeats of both Ouranos and Kronos began when their wives grew angry and took independent action as a result of their husbands' interference with the normal process of birth, and it certainly seems as though the scenario is about to be repeated in the third generation. But we hear no more about the matter from Hesiod, for whom Zeus is now and henceforth secure in his position as master of the universe, with all challenges past and overcome.

For a suggestion of conflict between Zeus on one side, and Hera and Hephaistos on the other, we must turn to the *Iliad*, which contains two contradictory versions of Hephaistos' relations with his parents. In *Iliad* 1.590-594, Hephaistos cautions his mother against continuing her quarrel with Zeus by reminding her that once before Zeus had ended a dispute by punishing her, and furthermore had thrown Hephaistos out of the sky:

At another time, when I tried to help you,
he seized my foot and threw me from the gods' threshold.
All day I fell, and with the setting sun
I landed on Lemnos, and little life was still in me;
after I fell, Sintian men rescued me.

In *Iliad* 18.395-398, however, Hephaistos contradicts his own earlier story and claims that he was thrown from the sky by Hera, who was ashamed of the lame child to whom she had given birth. In this version, Hephaistos falls not on the island of Lemnos but into the sea, where he is rescued by the goddesses Eurynome and Thetis:

> She [Thetis] saved me, when I suffered, falling far
> by the will of my dog-faced mother, who wanted to
> hide me since I was lame; then I would have suffered
> in spirit if Eurynome and Thetis had not received me.

The only thing these two versions have in common is Hephaistos' fall from the sky, while they differ in who threw him, when and why he was thrown, how he became lame, and who rescued him. And yet both versions could correspond with a hypothetical myth in which an angry Hera bore Hephaistos by herself in order to gain revenge on her husband. In the *Iliad* 18 version her plan is thwarted by the lameness of her parthenogenic son, whom she abandons when he does not live up to her expectations. In *Iliad* 1, however, Hephaistos seems to be playing the role of the oedipal rival on the recalled occasion when he fought against his father on behalf of his mother.

There may well have been a pre-Hesiodic theogonic variant in which Zeus had to defend his position and claim to permanent rule by overcoming a challenge brought by his own son. In this variant Zeus would have faced exactly the same sort of rebellion as those which undid his father and grandfather. Unlike them, he would have defeated his son and thrown him out of the sky (like Milton's Lucifer), and thus put an end to the cycle of oedipal succession.

While a remnant of this hypothetical myth may have survived in the *Iliad* 1 account of enmity between Zeus and Hephaistos, the Hesiodic tradition—perhaps Hesiod himself—chose to suppress it in favor of an alternate account of conflict between Zeus and a fire-god, the rebellion of Prometheus. There are many possible reasons why this displacement may have taken place, the most likely of which center on Hesiod's conception of the nature and role of Zeus (e.g., the desire to make Zeus' victory the result of wisdom rather than force), but the possibility that it took place is supported by a complex of evidence in the *Theogony* and other surviving Greek literature.

The connection between Hephaistos and Prometheus extends far beyond the underlying fact that they are both fire-gods; there are several other specific situations in which the two are closely related and sometimes functionally interchangeable. For example, there are versions in which Prometheus is called a son of Hera (scholia to *Iliad* 5.205, 14.295) and both Prometheus and Hephaistos are said to have fallen in love with Athena (scholia to Apollonios Rhodios 2.1249; *Ap* 3.14.6); both Hephaistos and Prometheus are said to have assisted at the birth of Athena from the head of

Zeus (Euripides, *Ion* 455; Pindar, *Olympian* 7.35); Hephaistos created Pandora by mixing earth and water (*Th* 571) and Prometheus was credited with the creation of mankind by the same means (*Ap* 1.7.1); both Hephaistos and Prometheus were honored as the bringers of culture and technical advancement to humanity (Aeschylus, *Prometheus Bound* 436-506; *Hh to Hephaistos* 2-7); Hephaistos was called the father or grandfather of the Lemnian Kabeiroi, and Prometheus was named as one of the Theban Kabeiroi (Strabo 10.3.21; Pausanias 9.25.6); in Attika the shrines and cults of Hephaistos and Prometheus were closely associated.

Given this network of associations, it is not difficult to see how Prometheus could replace Hephaistos as the defeated rival of Zeus, especially since the crime of Prometheus, the theft of fire, is an oedipal offense. And yet the conflict between Zeus and Prometheus is essentially concerned with cleverness and deceit, in which Prometheus regularly has the upper hand until finally Zeus tires of the game and consigns Prometheus to his cliff and man-eating eagle. There is nothing of the cosmic violence which marked the struggles of previous generations and which is suggested in the *Iliad* 1 account of the confrontation between Zeus and Hephaistos. For this aspect of Zeus' victory, we must turn to another Hephaistos-substitute, the monster Typhoeus.

Hesiod calls Typhoeus the son of Gaia and Tartaros, and does not mention any connection between the monster and Hera. In two other versions, however, Typhoeus is closely linked to Hera, her enmity with Zeus, and (either directly or indirectly) with Hephaistos. In one version (scholia to *Iliad* 2.783) Gaia, angered by the death of the Giants, complained to Hera, who asked Kronos for help. He gave her two eggs smeared with his semen and told her to bury them in the ground, predicting that from them would be born an avenger who could overthrow Zeus. She buried the eggs in Kilikia and Typhoeus was born, but Hera then was reconciled with Zeus; she told him what had happened and he killed Typhoeus with a thunderbolt.

In the other version (*Hh to Apollo* 305-356), Hera, angry because Zeus had produced Athena by himself whereas her own attempt at parthenogenesis had resulted in the crippled Hephaistos, whom she had thrown from the sky (as in *Iliad* 18), prayed to Gaia, Ouranos, and the Titans that she would bear a son greater than Zeus. A year later she gave birth to Typhoeus and entrusted him to the serpent Pytho to raise:

> Once she [Pytho] received from gold-throned Hera and raised
> terrible and cruel Typhoeus, a plague to mortals.   306
> Hera bore him since she was angry with father Zeus,
> when he, Kronos' son, bore illustrious Athena
> in his head; mistress Hera grew immediately angry

and spoke among the assembled immortals: 310
"Hear from me, all gods and goddesses,
how cloud-gatherer Zeus begins to dishonor me
unprovoked, after he made me his true and good wife.
Now without me he bore owl-eyed Athena,
who is eminent among all the blessed immortals.   315
But my son was born the weakest of all gods,
Hephaistos with crippled feet, whom I bore by myself.
I seized him and threw him into the wide sea.
But Nereus' daughter, silver-shod Thetis,
rescued and cared for him with her sisters;   320
she should have done some other favor for the blessed gods.
Bold and clever one, what else will you now plot?
How dared you bear owl-eyed Athena alone?
Would I not have borne a child? At least I am called
yours, among the immortals who possess the wide sky.   325
Take care I do not plot some future evil for you.
Even now I will arrange to give birth to a son,
who will be eminent among the immortal gods,
without disgracing the holy bed of you and me.
I will not come to your embrace, but going far   330
from you I will be with the immortal gods."
Saying this with angry heart she left the gods.
Then cow-eyed mistress Hera prayed at once,
struck the ground with flat hand, and said:
"Hear me now, Gaia and vast Ouranos above   335
and Titan gods who live under the earth
in great Tartaros, ancestors of men and gods.
All of you now listen and give me a son apart from
Zeus and just as strong as Zeus; rather, may he be
stronger, as wide-seeing Zeus is stronger than Kronos."   340
Saying this, she struck the earth with her great hand;
and life-bearing Gaia was moved; seeing this, she felt
joy in her heart, for she thought it would come to pass.
From then on until the year's completion
she never came to the bed of wise Zeus   345
nor to the carved chair, where formerly
she sat and planned dense counsels,
but she stayed in her crowded temples
and enjoyed her offerings, cow-eyed mistress Hera.
But when the months and days were fulfilled   350
and the seasons passed through the circling year,

she bore a child unlike gods or mortals,
terrible and cruel Typhoeus, a plague to mortals.
Quickly cow-eyed mistress Hera took and gave him
[to Pytho], one evil thing to another; and she received   355
him; and he did many wrongs to the famous races of men.

The most striking fact about this version is that Typhoeus is conceived by Hera in the same way and for the same reason that Hephaistos is conceived in *Theogony* 924-929. This version also gives us, in effect, the background of the *Iliad* 18 account (i.e., why Hera bore the crippled Hephaistos) and both versions provide the aftermath of the *Theogony* 927-929 account (i.e., what happened to Hephaistos after his parthenogenic birth). Although the *Theogony* does not mention Hera's ill-treatment of Hephaistos, and Homer in *Iliad* 18 does not mention a quarrel between Zeus and Hera, the two accounts along with the *Hymn to Apollo* seem unmistakably to represent a tradition in which Hera gave birth to Hephaistos in order to avenge herself against Zeus and in which Typhoeus and Hephaistos play similar roles.

If in fact these two major digressions in the *Theogony*, the episodes involving Prometheus and Typhoeus, are Hesiod's reworking of another version in which Zeus' final victory was over his own son, we may conclude with a few speculations concerning the motivation for this displacement.

Zeus, as Hesiod continually reminds us, is the ultimate paternal figure, the "father of gods and men." But this ultimate father is also a good father, who maintains his rule not by the defeat and punishment of his sons but by victory over a thief and a monster. He is totally unlike his father and grandfather, whose relationship with their sons was pure hostility and violence and who were implacably opposed to generation itself. Zeus, on the other hand, has the intelligence and, in a sense, sufficient self-restraint to avoid a repetition of the past.

Perhaps more importantly, the *Theogony* is concerned not so much with the present (that is, the unchanging present of the gods once Zeus has won dominion) as with the past and how things came to be as they are. It is in the present that Zeus is Father, and Hesiod shows us the implicit but certain logic of Zeus' ascent to permanent paternity and sovereignty. Underlying the logical inevitability of Zeus' triumph, however, is an emotional imperative of equal force, whose focus is not Zeus as idealized Father in the present but Zeus as idealized Son in the past. His triumph represents the replacement of fathers by their sons, and even his paternal role (i.e., endless procreation) is the wish-fulfilling result of his oedipal victory. He wins the fulfillment of divine sons' dreams—virtually unlimited sexual access to goddesses and women—and, thanks to his strategic observance of a small but significant exception to this availability (his swallowing of Metis and avoidance of Thetis), no ambitious son will appear to challenge his rule and take his place. If Hephaistos once was such a son, Hesiod has erased this fact and replaced it with Zeus' victories over Prometheus and Typhoeus, both of whom are associated primarily with the Titans and the older generation.

Zeus, the hero of Hesiod's vision, is the all-conquering son, the supreme example of an oedipal success story. In this myth, whose primary intellectual function is the description and explanation of the origin of the world and its gods, the narrative is impelled and energized by an emotional structure of symbiotic memories, oedipal wishes, and filial ambitions.

The story of Pandora provides an interesting example of this intellectual and emotional interaction. At first glance it might seem that the only emotional motivation present in the episode is misogyny, a view of women as at best a necessary evil and a great plague (*Theogony*), or as responsible for the presence of evil and suffering in the world and the necessity of labor (*Works and Days*). But if mortal woman is to be true to the divine precedents of the *Theogony*, she must be a "lovely evil" (*Th* 585) to her husband, since this is the role assumed by the divine wives in the succession story. If sons overthrow their fathers, it is not only because that is the way things are but also, and specifically, because mothers favor their sons. If women appear as dangerous and evil in the story of Pandora, this is simply an extension of the roles of Gaia and Rhea, whose maternal allegiances regularly turn them against their husbands. From the viewpoint of the son, the good mother is necessarily a bad wife, since she must take the side of her son against her husband. And the viewpoint of the son is the viewpoint of the *Theogony*.

APPENDIX A

Hesiod, *Works and Days*, Lines 1-201

The *Works and Days* is a didactic poem of 828 lines, most of which are concerned with advice and instruction on agriculture, seafaring, and moral and practical conduct. These exhortations are addressed to Hesiod's brother Perses, who is said to have cheated Hesiod out of his fair share of his inheritance, and at times to the "kings" whom Perses bribed in his evil plan. All of the poem is of great interest, but only the first 201 lines are concerned with mythical topics. First is the myth of Prometheus and Pandora (47-105), a revised version of the same story told in the *Theogony*, and second is the myth of the Five Races, a history of the devolution of mankind from its original symbiotic bliss to its present miserable condition.

Muses of Pieria,° who glorify with song,
Come, tell of your father Zeus in song;
Thanks to him mortal men are both famous and obscure,
known and unknown, by the will of great Zeus.
easily he makes one strong, easily he crushes the strong,   5
easily he lowers the high and raises the lowly,
easily straightens the crooked and withers the proud,
high-thundering Zeus whose home is most high.
hear me, see and listen, straighten decrees with justice;
and I would tell the truth to Perses.   10
There was not one birth of Eris,° but on earth
there are two; who knows the one would praise her,
but the other is to be blamed; they have opposite minds.
One advances evil war and battle, the cruel one;
no mortal loves her, but of necessity they honor   15
the harsh Eris, by the will of the immortals.
The other was born first to dark Nyx, and
Kronos' son, who dwells in brightness, high-throned,
put her in earth's roots and made her better for men;
she rouses even the helpless to work.   20
For a man wanting work, when he sees another
who is rich, who hurries to plow and plant and

---

1 For Pieria see on *Th* 54
11 Eris is Discord (*Th* 225).

arrange his affairs well, is envious of his neighbor
who hurries after wealth; this Eris is good for mortals.
So potter is at odds with potter, and artisan with artisan, 25
beggar resents beggar, and singer envies singer.
Perses, put these things in your heart,
lest evil-loving Eris check your heart from work
as you spy on disputes and listen at court.
For disputes and courts barely concern a man 30
whose year's livelihood is not stored up at home
on time, that which the earth bears, Demeter's grain.
If you have that in abundance, advance disputes and strife
for another's goods. There will be no second time
for you to do this, but let us now settle the quarrel 35
with straight judgments, which are of Zeus and best.
For we divided our inheritance before, and you seized
and carried off much else, greatly flattering the
gift-eating kings who want to make this judgment,
fools who do not know how much the half exceeds 40
the whole, and what a great good is mallow and asphodel.
For the gods hide and hold man's means of life;
or you would easily accomplish enough in a day
to keep you for a year, even without working;
you would quickly store the rudder over the smoke, 45
the work of oxen and hard-working mules would perish.
But Zeus hid this, angered in his heart,
because crafty Prometheus deceived him.
Therefore he contrived miserable cares for men;
ge hid fire; but the fine son of Iapetos 50
stole it back for men from wise Zeus in a
hollow narthex, deceiving thunder-loving Zeus.
Cloud-gatherer Zeus was angered and said to him,
"Son of Iapetos, knowing thoughts beyond all,
you rejoice, having stolen fire and seduced my mind, 55
a great woe to you yourself and to men who will be.
I will give them an evil to pay for fire, which all
might enjoy at heart, embracing their own evil."
So he spoke, and the father of men and gods laughed.
He ordered famous Hephaistos immediately 60
to mix earth with water, and to put in a human voice
and strength, to make it like immortal goddesses in face,
a beautiful, lovely maiden's image; and Athena

to teach her crafts, to weave the skillful web;
and golden Aphrodite to pour charm over her head,   65
and terrible longing and limb-consuming cares;
and he ordered Hermes Argeiphontes,° the messenger,
to put in her a bitch's mind and deceiving behavior.
So he spoke, and they obeyed lord Zeus, Kronos' son.
Quickly the famous Lame One° made from earth the   70
likeness of a modest virgin, by the plans of Kronos' son;
owl-eyed Athena sashed her and dressed her;
the divine Charites and mistress Peitho° put
golden necklaces on her skin, and on her head the
lovely-haired Horai put a garland of spring flowers;   75
and Pallas Athene arranged all the finery on her skin.
And in her heart the messenger Argeiphontes
put lies and sly stories and deceitful behavior,
by the plans of deep-sounding Zeus; the herald
of the gods put in a voice, and named this woman   80
Pandora, since all who have Olympian homes
presented a gift, a woe to men who work for food.
And when he finished the sheer irresistible trick,
the father sent famed Argeiphontes, the gods' swift
messenger, to take the gift to Epimetheus; and Epimetheus   85
did not think about what Prometheus told him, never
to accept a gift from Olympian Zeus, but to send it
back, lest it turn out to be some evil for mortals.
But he took it, and knew the evil only when he had it.
For earlier the tribes of men used to live on the earth   90
free and apart from evils and without hard trouble
and harsh diseases which bring doom to men;   92
but the woman opened the jar's great lid with her hands,   94
and scattered these; she wrought sad cares for men.   95
Elpis° alone, there in the unbreakable home,
stayed within under the jar's rim, and did not
fly out; for before this she closed the jar's lid
by the plans of cloud-gatherer Zeus Aigiochos.
But the rest, uncounted miseries, wander among men;   100

---

67 Argeiphontes, an epithet of Hermes, probably means "Dog-Slayer" (West, *WD* 368-369).

70 The "Lame One" is Hephaistos.

73 The Charites are the Graces; Peitho is Persuasion.

96 Elpis is Hope.

the earth is full of evils, the sea is full;
by day and by night spontaneous diseases
visit men, bringing evils to mortals in
silence, since wise Zeus took away their voice.
So there is no way to escape the mind of Zeus.   105
    If you wish, I will relate another story to you,
well and knowingly, and do you put it in your heart,
how gods and mortal men are born from the same.
First a golden race of mortal men were
made by the immortals who have Olympian homes.   110
They lived in Kronos' time, when he ruled the sky;
they lived like gods, with carefree heart,
free and apart from trouble and pain; grim old age
did not afflict them, but with legs and arms always
strong they played in delight, apart from all evils;   115
They died as if subdued by sleep; and all good things
were theirs; the fertile earth produced fruit
by itself, abundantly and unforced; willingly and
effortlessly they ruled their lands with many goods.
[rich in flocks and dear to the blessed gods]   120
But since the earth hid this race below,
they are daimones° by the plans of great Zeus,
benevolent earthly guardians of mortal men,
[who watch over judgments and cruel deeds,
clothed in air and roaming over all the earth]   125
wealth-givers; they also hold this kingly right.
Afterwards a second, much worse age of
silver was made by those who have Olympian homes,
not like the golden in body and mind.
For a hundred years a child was raised by his   130
dear mother, a great fool playing in his house;
but when they grew up and reached youth's measure,
they would live but a short time, having griefs
in their foolishness; for they could not restrain
rash violence from one another, and they did not want   135
to serve the immortals or sacrifice on the holy altars
of the blessed, as is right for men by custom. Then
Kronos' son Zeus was angry and hid them, since they
would not give honors to the gods who hold Olympos.

---

122 Daimones are spirits who watch over mortals, mysterious, invisible, and virtually
anonymous.

But since the earth also hid this race below,   140
they are called blessed mortals under the earth;
they are second, but still honor attends them.
Father Zeus made a third race of mortal men
of bronze, not at all like the silver,
from ash-trees, terrible and strong, who cared for   145
the grievous works of Ares and violence; they ate
no bread, but had a hard-hearted spirit of adamant;
they were unformed; great strength and unbeatable arms
grew from their shoulders over mighty limbs.
Bronze was their armor, bronze their houses,   150
with bronze they worked; black iron did not exist.
And conquered by their own hands
they went to the moldy house of icy Hades,
nameless; although they were mighty, black death
seized them, and they left the sun's shining light.   155
But when the earth also hid this race below,
still another, the fourth on the fertile earth,
was made by Kronos' son Zeus, more just and better,
a godlike race of heroes who are called demi-gods,
the race before ours on the boundless earth.   160
Evil war and the grim din of battle destroyed
them, some below seven-gated Thebes, in the Kadmeian
land, fighting over the flocks of Oidipous, and
leading some in ships over the sea's great gulf
to Troy, for the sake of rich-haired Helene.   165
There death's end covered over some of them,
but, giving to others a life and home apart from men,
Kronos' son, father Zeus, settled them at the ends of the   168
earth, and they dwell, with carefree heart, in the   170
islands of the blessed by deep-whirling Okeanos;
happy heroes, for whom the fertile earth bears
honey-sweet fruit, ripe, three times a year.
[they are far from the immortals; Kronos is their king   173a
] the father of men and gods released him;   173b
[Now] he has honor among them as [is fitting.   173c
But Zeus] made another race [of mortal men,   173d
of those who now] are born on [the fertile earth.]   173e
    I wish I were not among the fifth   174
men, but died before or was born later.   175
For now the race is of iron; never by day

will they cease from labor and pain, nor by night
from being oppressed; the gods will give harsh cares.
But still, even for them good will be mixed with evil.
And Zeus will destroy this race of mortal men too,   180
when at birth they are grey at the temples.
A father will not agree with his children, nor children
with their father, nor guest with host or comrade with
comrade, nor will brother be friend to brother, as before.
They will be quick to dishonor aging parents;   185
they will find fault with them, speaking harsh words,
cruel, ignorant of the gods' vengeance; nor will
they repay aging parents for their nurture.
Might will be right; one will sack another's city;
there will be no appreciation of the man who keeps   190
his word, or is just or good, but they will honor instead
the evil-doer and violent man; justice and respect
will be in violence; the evil man will harm the better,
saying crooked words, and will swear an oath on it.
Zelos° will accompany all the sorry men,   195
bringing disturbance, loving evil, hate-faced.
And then to Olympos, from the wide-pathed earth,
concealing their beautiful skin in white robes,
abandoning men for the race of the immortals,
Aidos and Nemesis° will go; miserable pains will   200
be left for mortal men, there will be no cure of evil.

---

195 Zelos is the personification of Envy.
200 Aidos [Reverence] is internally-imposed restraint; Nemesis [Retribution, Indigna-
tion] is externally-imposed restraint.

Appendix B

The Library of Apollodoros

We do not know who wrote the collection of Greek myths usually referred to as the *Bibliotheke*, or *Library*, of Apollodoros the Athenian, nor do we know when it was written, although most scholars would date it to the first or second century A.D. There are many references in ancient writings to the work of an eminent Athenian grammarian named Apollodoros who lived in the 2nd century B.C., but it seems for various reasons impossible that this Apollodoros was the author of the *Library*, which, as far as we know, is mentioned by no dated author earlier than Photius in the 9th century A.D.

The mystery of its date and the anonymity of its author are, in a sense, appropriate for the *Library*. No matter when it was actually written, it represents that hypothetical point in history when Greek myth became a mythological system, fixed for all time. Some, including perhaps the Greeks themselves, might identify this point as the time of Hesiod and Homer, or even long before; others might date it to the end of the 5th century, when the demise of Greek tragedy crystallized the myths in their most familiar, although often contradictory, variants. Although the almost twenty sources cited by him range from Hesiod and Homer in the 8th century to Castor in the 1st century, the passage of time does not mean that myths change; it merely allows different versions to arise of what actually happened in that period before Hesiod when the events of myth took place.

The personality of the author of the *Library*, like the date at which he wrote, is completely transcended by his subject. Although preceded by a long tradition of scholarly writing on Greek myth, works which attempted either to interpret myths (e.g., Herodoros, Euhemeros, Palaiphatos) or to insert them into the history of cities or peoples (e.g., Hekataios, Akousilaos, Pherekydes), the *Library* has no purpose other than the orderly account of the totality of Greek myths in and for themselves. There is no attempt to evaluate or criticize or interpret the mythical material, nor is there any perceptible literary or artistic intention.

The following passages are excerpted from Book One of the *Library*.

1.1.1. Ouranos [Sky], the first ruler of the whole world, married Gaia [Earth]. His first children were Briareos, Gyges, and Kottos, who are called the Hundred-Handed and were unsurpassed in size and power, each having one hundred hands and fifty heads.

1.1.2. After these, Gaia bore to him the Kyklopes, each with one eye on his forehead, Arges, Steropes, and Brontes. Ouranos however bound these and threw them into Tartaros (this is a dark place in Hades, as far away from earth as earth is from sky).

1.1.3. Ouranos again had children by Gaia: the sons, called Titans, were Okeanos, Koios, Hyperion, Kreios, Iapetos, and Kronos, the youngest; the daughters, called Titanides, were Tethys, Rhea, Themis, Mnemosyne, Phoibe, Dione, and Theia.

1.1.4. Gaia, angered by the loss of her children who had been thrown into Tartaros, persuaded the Titans to attack their father and gave an adamantine sickle to Kronos. All but Okeanos took part in the attack, and Kronos cut off his father's genitals and threw them into the sea; Alekto, Tisiphone, and Megaira, the Erinyes [Furies], were born from the drops of flowing blood. After deposing Ouranos, they brought back their brothers who had been thrown into Tartaros and entrusted the rule to Kronos.

1.1.5. But he bound them and imprisoned them again in Tartaros, and married his sister Rhea. Since both Gaia and Ouranos prophesied to him that his rule would be usurped by his own son, he would swallow his children as they were born. He swallowed Hestia, the first-born, then Demeter and Hera, and after them Plouton and Poseidon.

1.1.6. Angered by this, Rhea went to Crete when she happened to be pregnant with Zeus. The baby was born in a cave of Dikte and entrusted by his mother for nurturance to the Kouretes and the nymphs Adrasteia and Ida, daughters of Melisseus.

1.1.7. The nymphs therefore nursed the child with the milk of Amaltheia, while the Kouretes, in arms, guarded the baby in the cave by striking their shields with their spears, so that Kronos would not hear the child's voice. Rhea meanwhile wrapped a stone in a blanket as though it were a new-born child and gave it to Kronos to swallow.

1.2.1. When Zeus was full-grown, he acquired the assistance of Metis, the daughter of Okeanos; she gave Kronos a drug to swallow, by which he was compelled to disgorge first the stone, then the children he had swallowed. With their help Zeus carried on the war against Kronos and the Titans. After they had fought for ten years, Gaia prophesied victory to Zeus if he would have as allies those who had been thrown into Tartaros. He therefore killed Kampe, the custodian of their chains, and released them. The Kyklopes then gave Zeus thunder and lightning and the thunderbolt; and they gave a helmet to Plouton and a trident to Poseidon. Armed with these they conquered the Titans, shut them up in Tartaros, and appointed the Hundred-Handed as guards. As for themselves, they cast lots for the rule;

Zeus obtained the kingship of the sky, Poseidon that of the sea, and Plouton that of Hades.

1.2.2. These are the descendants of the Titans: the children of Okeanos and Tethys were Asia, Styx, Elektra, Doris, Eurynome, and Metis, the Okeanids; the children of Koios and Phoibe were Asteria and Leto; the children of Hyperion and Theia were Eos [Dawn], Helios [Sun], and Selene [Moon]; the children of Kreios and Eurybia, daughter of Pontos [Sea], were Astraios, Pallas, and Perses.

1.2.3. The children of Iapetos and Asia were Atlas, who holds the sky on his shoulders, Prometheus, Epimetheus, and Menoitios, who was struck by Zeus' thunderbolt during the Titanomachy [Titan-War] and thrown down to Tartaros.

1.2.4. The child of Kronos and Philyra was Cheiron, a centaur of double nature; the children of Eos and Astraios were the winds and stars; the child of Perses and Asteria was Hekate; the children of Pallas and Styx were Nike, Kratos, Zelos, and Bia.

1.2.5. The water of Styx, which flows from a rock in Hades, was made by Zeus into an object by which oaths were sworn; he gave this honor to Styx because she and her children had fought against the Titans with him.

1.2.6. The children of Pontos and Gaia were Phorkys, Thaumas, Nereus, Eurybia, and Keto. The children of Thaumas and Elektra were Iris and the Harpies, Aello and Okypete; the children of Phorkys and Keto were the Phorkides and the Gorgons (of whom we shall speak when we relate the adventures of Perseus).

1.2.7. The children of Nereus and Doris were the Nereids, whose names were Kymothoe, Speio, Glaukonome, Nausithoe, Halia, Erato, Sao, Amphitrite, Eunike, Thetis, Eulimene, Agaue, Eudora, Doto, Pherousa, Galateia, Aktaia, Pontomedousa, Hippothoe, Lysianassa, Kymo, Eione, Halimede, Plexaura, Eukrante, Proto, Kalypso, Panope, Kranto, Neomeris, Hipponoe, Ianeira, Polynome, Autonoe, Melite, Dione, Nesaia, Dero, Euagore, Psamathe, Eumolpe, Ione, Dynamene, Keto, and Limnoreia.

1.3.1. Zeus married Hera and became the father of Hebe, Eileithyia, and Ares, but he had sexual relations with many women, both mortal and immortal. His daughters by Themis, the daughter of Ouranos, were the Horai: Eirene [Peace], Eunomia [Order], and Dike [Justice]; and the Moirai: Klotho, Lachesis, and Atropos. By Dione he had Aphrodite; by Eurynome, daughter of Okeanos, he had the Charites: Aglaia, Euphrosyne, and Thaleia; by Styx he had Persephone; by Mnemosyne he had the Muses: first Kalliope, then Kleio, Melpomene, Euterpe, Erato, Terpsichore, Ourania, Thaleia, and Polymnia.

1.3.5. Hera gave birth to Hephaistos without having had sexual intercourse, but Homer says that she bore him to Zeus. When Hephaistos came to help his bound mother, Zeus threw him out of the sky; for Zeus had hung Hera from Olympos when she sent a storm against Herakles, who was at sea after capturing Troy. Hephaistos fell on Lemnos and his feet were crippled, but Thetis saved him.

1.3.6. Although Metis changed into many shapes in order to avoid a sexual encounter, Zeus had intercourse with her. When she became pregnant, he quickly swallowed her since she said that, after the daughter to whom she was about to give birth, she would bear a son who would be the ruler of the sky. This is what Zeus feared when he swallowed Metis. When it was time for the birth to take place, Prometheus (or, as others say, Hephaistos) struck the head of Zeus with an axe; and Athena leaped up from the top of his head with her weapons, at the river Triton.

1.4.6. Poseidon married Amphitrite, and there were born to him Triton and Rhode, who became the wife of Helios.

1.6.1. Gaia, who was angry because of the Titans, gave birth to the Giants by Ouranos; these were insuperable in size and strength, and frightening in appearance, with long hair falling from their heads and chins, and the scales of dragons for feet. They were born, as some say, in Phlegrai, but others say that they were born in Pallene. They would throw rocks and flaming oaks at the sky. Porphyrion surpassed the rest, and so did Alkyoneus, who was immortal while fighting in the land where he was born. He also drove the cattle of Helios from Erytheia. The gods had an oracle that none of the Giants could be killed by the gods, but would die if a certain mortal was the ally of the gods. Gaia learned this and searched for an herbal drug, so that they could not be killed by a mortal. Zeus commanded Eos, Selene, and Helios [Dawn, Moon, and Sun] not to shine, and he was the first to pick the herb; he then had Athena summon Herakles to be his ally. Herakles first shot Alkyoneus, but when he fell on the ground he began to revive; at Athena's suggestion, Herakles dragged him out of Pallene and thus he died.

1.6.2. Porphyrion attacked both Herakles and Hera in the battle. But Zeus caused him to lust after Hera; when he tore her clothes, wanting to rape her, she called for help. Zeus struck him with a thunderbolt and Herakles killed him with an arrow. As for the rest, Apollo shot Ephialtes with an arrow in the left eye, and Herakles shot him in the right eye; Dionysos killed Eurytos with his thyrsos; Hekate killed Klytios with torches; Hephaistos killed Mimas with searing metal; Athena threw the island of Sicily on Enkelados as he fled and stripped off the skin of Pallas to protect her in battle; Poseidon, having pursued Polybotes through the sea until he came to the island of Kos, tore off the part of the island called Nisyron and threw it on him; Hermes, wearing the cap of Hades, killed Hippolytos in the battle; Artemis killed Aigaion; the Moirai, fighting with bronze clubs, killed Agrios and Thoas; Zeus killed the rest by striking them with thunderbolts, and Herakles shot them all with arrows as they died.

1.6.3. When the gods had conquered the Giants, Gaia became angrier; she had intercourse with Tartaros and gave birth in Kilikia to Typhon, who had the combined nature of man and beast. In size and strength he surpassed all the sons of Gaia; from the thighs upward, he had a human shape of such immense size that he towered over all the mountains and his head often touched the stars. One of his hands stretched toward evening and the other stretched toward dawn; from them projected a hundred serpent's heads. From the thighs downward, he had great coils of vipers which hissed loudly and, when uncoiled, reached up to his head. Wings covered his entire body, squalid hair on his head and jaw blew in the wind, and he flashed fire from his eyes. This was the appearance and size of Typhon when, hissing and shouting and throwing burning rocks, he made his way to the sky itself; from his mouth he sent a great spray of fire. When the gods saw him rushing toward the sky, they fled to Egypt and, being pursued, changed their shapes into animals. Zeus struck Typhon with thunderbolts when he was far off; when he was close, he struck him down with an adamantine sickle, and pursued him as he fled to Mount Kasios, which is situated above Syria. There Zeus saw that he was wounded and wrestled with him. But Typhon entangled him in his coils and held him; seizing the sickle and cutting the sinews of his hands and feet, he hoisted him on his shoulders and brought him through the sea to Kilikia where he put him down in the Korykian cave. Having hidden the sinews in a bear-skin he left them there also, and stationed as a guard the she-serpent Delphyne, a virgin who was half-beast. Hermes and Aigipan, however, stole the sinews and fitted them to Zeus without being seen. When he had recovered his former strength, he suddenly came riding in a chariot of winged horses from the sky and, throwing thunderbolts, pursued Typhon to the mountain called Nysa, where the Moirai deceived him in his flight; for he tasted the ephemeral fruit, having been persuaded that his strength would be increased. Therefore, again being pursued, he came to Thrace, and while fighting around Haimos he threw whole mountains. When these were thrust back at him by the thunderbolt, a quantity of blood streamed out from the mountain, and they say that the mountain is called Haimos for this reason. When he hastened to flee through the Sicilian sea, Zeus threw Aitna, a mountain in Sicily, on him. This mountain is of great size and to this day they say that eruptions of fire from it are due to the thunderbolts which were thrown.

1.7.1. I have now said enough about that matter. Prometheus, having made men from water and earth, also gave them fire, hiding it in a fennel-stalk without the knowledge of Zeus. When Zeus learned of this, he ordered Hephaistos to nail Prometheus' body to Mount Caucasus, a Skythian mountain on which he was fastened and confined for many years. Each day an eagle flew down and fed on the lobes of his liver, which grew during the night. Prometheus paid this penalty for the stolen fire until Herakles later released him.

1.7.2 A son of Prometheus was Deukalion, who was king of the area around Phthia and married Pyrrha, daughter of Epimetheus and Pandora, the first woman created by the gods. When Zeus wished to obliterate the Bronze Age, Deukalion, at the suggestion of Prometheus, built an ark, put supplies in it, and embarked with Pyrrha. Zeus poured a great amount of heavy rain from the sky and flooded most areas of Hellas, so that all men were destroyed except for the few who fled to the high mountaintops nearby. At this time also, the mountains in Thessaly divided, and all areas outside the Isthmus and the Peloponnese were flooded. Deukalion, carried through the sea in the ark for nine days and nights, landed at Parnassos, and there, when the rain stopped, he disembarked and sacrificed to Zeus Phyxios. Zeus sent Hermes to him and ordered him to choose whatever he wished, and he chose to have men. Zeus told him to pick up stones and throw them over his head; those which Deukalion threw became men and those which Pyrrha threw became women. For this reason "people" were metaphorically named laoi from laas, the word for "stone."

1.7.3. The children of Deukalion and Pyrrha were, first, Hellen, who some say was a son of Zeus; second, Amphiktyon, who was king of Attika after Kranaos; and a daughter Protogeneia, the mother by Zeus of Aithlios. The children of Hellen and the nymph Orseis were Doros, Xouthos, and Aiolos. He named those who were called Greeks "Hellenes" after himself, and he divided the country among his sons. The children of Xouthos, who received the Peloponnese, and Kreousa, the daughter of Erechtheus, were Achaios and Ion, for whom the Achaians and Ionians are named. Doros, who received the land beyond the Peloponnese, named the inhabitants Dorians after himself, and Aiolos, who was king of the region around Thessaly, called the inhabitants Aiolians.

INDEX

References are to pages in the text except: following *Th* when they refer to line numbers in the *Theogony*, following *Ap* when they refer to sections in the *Library*, following *WD* when they refer to lines in the *Works and Days*. A lowercase 'n' indicates references to footnotes in the *Theogony* (*Th*) or *Works and Days* (*WD*). Names are identified in parentheses; Latin spellings are provided in braces.

Eurytion (a herdsman), *Th* 293; *Th* 289-294n
Eurytos (a Giant), *Ap* 1.6.2
Euterpe (one of the Muses), 11; *Th* 77; *Th* 75-79n; *Ap* 1.3.1
Five Races, 14, 105
Gaia [Gaea] (Earth), 2-10, 14-5, 23, 24, 26, 89, 90-1, 94-7, 100, 101, 103; *Th* 20, 45, 106, 117, 126, 147, 154, 158, 159, 172, 173, 176, 184, 238, 421, 463, 470, 479, 494, 505, 626, 644, 821, 858, 884, 891; *Th* 20n, 106-107n, 117-118n, 123n, 126-128n, 131-132n, 133-137n, 133n, 154-160n, 163-175n, 178-187n, 207-210n, 215-216n, 233-336n, 332-335n, 375n, 463-465n, 468-476n, 494-496n, 626-628n, 636n, 820-868n, 822n, 881-885n, 886-900n, 889-891; *Hh to Apollo* 335, 342; *Ap* 1.1.1, 1.1.2, 1.1.3, 1.1.4, 1.1.5, 1.2.1, 1.2.6, 1.6.1, 1.6.3
Galateia (a Nereid), *Th* 250; *Th* 250n, 243-264n; *Ap* 1.2.7
Galaxaura (one of the Kourai), *Th* 353
Galene (a Nereid), *Th* 244
Ganymedes (beautiful boy, raped by Zeus), *Th* 984-991n
Geras (Old Age, offspring of Night), 6, *Th* 225; *Th* 212-232n, 225n
Geryoneus (three-headed monster), 5, 7; *Th* 287, 289, 309, 982; *Th* 287-288n, 289-294n, 979-983n
Giants (born from blood of Ouranos), 6, 24, 100; *Th* 50, 185; *Th* 50n, 178-187n, 514-516n, 626-628n, 667n, 822n; *Ap* 1.6.1, 1.6.3
Glauke (a Nereid), *Th* 244
Glaukonome (a Nereid), *Th* 256; *Ap* 1.2.7
Glaukos, *Th* 233-236n
Gorgons (daughters of Phorkys and Keto), 5, 9; *Th* 274; *Th* 162n, 270-273n, 274-276n, 278-279n; *Ap* 1.2.6
Graiai [Graeae] (daughters of Phorkys and Keto), 7; *Th* 271; *Th* 270-273n
Granikos (a River), *Th* 342; *Th* 337-345n
Gyges (a Hundred-Handed), 5; *Th* 149, 618, 714, 734, 817; *Th* 147-153n; *Ap* 1.1.1
Hades, 9, 10, 11, 12, 13; *Th* 311, 455, 768, 774, 850; *Th* 119n, 138n, 310-312n, 454n, 455n, 720-819n, 885n, 912-914n, 930n; *WD* 153; *Ap* 1.1.2, 1.2.1, 1.2.5, 1.6.2
Halia (a Nereid), *Ap* 1.2.7
Haliakmon (a River), *Th* 341; *Th* 337-345n
Halimede (a Nereid), *Th* 255; *Ap* 1.2.7
Harmonia (daughter of Ares and Aphrodite, wife of Kadmos), 12; *Th* 937, 975; *Th* 933-937n, 940-942n, 975-978n
Harpies (daughters of Thaumas and Elektra), 7; *Th* 267; *Th* 267-269n, 295-303n; *Ap* 1.2.6

Hebe (Youth, daughter of Zeus and Hera), 11, 12; *Th* 17, 922, 952; *Th* 17n, 836-838n, 921-923n, 950-955n; *Ap* 1.3.1
Hekate [Hecate], *vii*, 8, 9, 10, 13, 14; *Th* 411, 418, 441; *Th* 376n, 411-452n, 440-447n, 450-452n, 454n; *Ap* 1.2.4, 1.6.2
Helene (wife of Menelaos, stolen away by Paris of Troy), *WD* 165
Helios [Helius] (Sun, son of Theia and Hyperion) 8, 12; *Th* 19, 372, 760, 956, 958, 1011; *Th* 19n, 133-137n, 207-210n, 371-374n, 756-766n, 956-962n, 984-991n; *Ap* 1.2.2, 1.4.6, 1.6.1
Hellen (son of Deukalion and Pyrrha, ancestor of the Hellenes), *Ap* 1.7.3
Hemera (Day, offspring of Erebos and Nyx), 5, 6; *Th* 124, 748; *Th* 124-145n, 720-819n, 748-754n
Hephaistos [Hephaestus], 4, 11, 12, 94, 98-103; *Th* 866, 928, 945; *Th* 11n, 139-146n, 244n, 358n, 454n, 513n, 565-567n, 570-589n, 571-572n, 573n, 820-868n, 886-900n, 907-911n, 924-926n; *Hh to Apollo* 317; *WD* 60; *WD* 70n; *Ap* 1.3.5, 1.3.6, 1.6.2, 1.7.1
Heptaporos (a River), *Th* 341; *Th* 337-345n
Hera, 4, 5, 9, 11, 12, 19, 91, 94, 96-99, 103; *Th* 11, 314, 328, 454, 921, 927, 952; *Th* 11n, 12n, 17n, 244n, 313-318n, 358n, 454n, 822n, 836-838n, 886-900n, 921-923n, 927-929n, 930n, 923n, 950-955n; *Hh to Apollo* 305, 307, 309, 333, 349, 354; *Ap* 1.1.5, 1.3.1, 1.3.5, 1.6.2
Herakles [Heracles], 10, 12; *Th* 289, 315, 316, 332, 526, 530, 943, 951, 982; *Th* 50n, 56-60n, 162n, 215-216n, 233-236n, 289-294n, 310-312n, 313-318n, 327-332n, 526-534n, 616n, 921-923n, 950-955n, 984-991n, 1003-1005n; *Ap* 1.3.5, 1.6.1, 1.6.2
Hermes, 19; *Th* 444, 938; *Th* 573n, 722-725n, 938-939n, 984-991n; *WD* 67; *Ap* 1.6.2, 1.6.3, 1.7.2
Hermos (a River), *Th* 343; *Th* 337-345n
Hesperethousa (one of the Hesperides), *Th* 215-216n
Hesperides (Daughters of Nyx) 6; *Th* 215 276, 518; *Th* 212-232n, 215-216n, 233-236n, 274-276n, 289-294n, 332-335n, 521-525n, 526-534n
Hestia (daughter of Kronos and Rhea) 9; *Th* 454; *Th* 454n; *Ap* 1.1.5
Himeros (Longing), *Th* 64, 201; *Th* 64n, 201n
Hippo (one of the Kourai), *Th* 351; *Th* 351n
Hippokrene (a spring on Mt Helikon), *Th* 6; *Th* 5-6n

Near Eastern Names

Geographical and Historical Names